BECH: A BOOK

John Updike

BECH:
A BOOK

Alfred A. Knopf   New York

Foreword

DEAR JOHN,

Well, if you must commit the artistic indecency of writing about a writer, better I suppose about me than about you. Except, reading along in these, I wonder if it *is* me, enough me, purely me. At first blush, for example, in Bulgaria (eclectic sexuality, bravura narcissism, thinning curly hair), I sound like some gentlemanly Norman Mailer; then that London glimpse of *silver* hair glints more of gallant, glamorous Bellow, the King of the Leprechauns, than of stolid old homely yours truly. My childhood seems out of Alex Portnoy and my ancestral past out of I. B. Singer. I get a whiff of Malamud in your city breezes, and am I paranoid to feel my "block" an ignoble version of the more or less noble renunciations of H. Roth, D. Fuchs, and J. Salinger? Withal, something Waspish, theological, scared, and insulatingly ironical that derives, my wild surmise is, from you.

Yet you are right. This monotonous hero who disembarks from an airplane, mouths words he doesn't quite mean, has vaguely to do with some woman, and gets back on the airplane, is certainly one Henry Bech. Until your short yet still not unlongish collection, no revolutionary has concerned himself with our oppression, with the silken mechanism whereby America reduces her writers to imbecility and cozenage. Envied like Negroes, disbelieved in like angels, we veer between the harlotry of the lecture platform and the torture of the writing desk, only to collapse, our five-and-dime Hallowe'en priests' robes a-rustle with economy-class jet-set tickets and honorary certificates from the Cunt-of-the-Month Club, amid a standing crowd of rueful, Lilliputian obituaries. Our language degenerating in the mouths of broadcasters and pop yellers, our formal designs crumbling like sand castles under the feet of beach bullies, we nevertheless and incredibly support with our desperate efforts (just now, I had to look up "desperate" in the dictionary for the ninety-ninth time, forgetting again if it is spelled with two "a"s or three "e"s) a flourishing culture of publishers, agents, editors, tutors, *Time*niks, media personnel in all shades of suavity, *chic*, and sexual gusto. When I think of the matings, the moaning, jubilant fornications between ectomorphic oversexed junior editors and svelte hot-from-Wellesley majored-in-English-minored-in-philosophy female coffee-fetchers and receptionists that have been engineered with the lever of some of my poor scratched-up and pasted-over pages (they arrive in the editorial offices as stiff with Elmer's glue as a masturbator's bedsheet; the office boys use them for tea-trays), I could mutilate myself like sainted Origen, I could keen like Jeremiah. Thank Jahweh these bordellos in the sky can soon dispense with the excuse of us entirely; already the contents of a book count as little as the contents of a breakfast cereal box. It is all a matter of the premium, and the shelf site, and the amount of air between the corn flakes. Never you mind. I'm sure that when with that blithe goyische brass I will never cease to grovel at you approached me for a "word or two by way of preface," you were bargaining for a benediction, not a curse.

Here it is, then. My blessing. I like some of the things in these accounts very much. The Communists are all good—good *people*. There is a moment by the sea, I've lost the page, that rang true. Here and there passages seemed overedited, constipated; you prune yourself too hard. With prose, there is no way to get it out, I have found, but to let it run. I liked some of the women you gave me, and a few of the jokes. By the way, I never—unlike retired light-verse writers—make puns. But if you [*here followed a list of suggested deletions, falsifications, suppressions, and rewordings, all of which have been scrupulously incorporated—*ED.], I don't suppose your publishing this little *jeu* of a book will do either of us drastic harm.

HENRY BECH

Manhattan,
Dec. 4th–12th, 1969

Contents

BECH: A BOOK

Rich in Russia

Students (not unlike yourselves) compelled to buy paperback copies of his novels—notably the first, *Travel Light*, though there has lately been some academic interest in his more surreal and "existential" and perhaps even "anarchist" second novel, *Brother Pig*—or encountering some essay from *When the Saints* in a shiny heavy anthology of mid-century literature costing $12.50, imagine that Henry Bech, like thousands less famous than he, is rich. He is not. The paperback rights to *Travel Light* were sold by his publisher outright for two thousand dollars, of which the publisher kept one thousand and Bech's agent one hundred (10% of 50%). To be fair, the publisher had had to remainder a third of the modest hard-cover printing and, when *Travel Light* was enjoying its vogue as the post-Golding pre-Tolkien fad of college undergraduates, would amusingly tell on himself the story of Bech's given-away rights, at

13

sales meetings upstairs in "21." As to anthologies—
the average permissions fee, when it arrives at Bech's
mailbox, has been eroded to $64.73, or some such
suspiciously odd sum, which barely covers the cost
of a restaurant meal with his mistress and a medium
wine. Though Bech, and his too numerous interviewers, have made a quixotic virtue of his continuing to live for twenty years in a grim if roomy
Riverside Drive apartment building (the mailbox,
students should know, where his pitifully nibbled
checks arrive has been well scarred by floating urban
wrath, and his last name has been so often ball-
pointed by playful lobby-loiterers into a somewhat
assonant verb that Bech has left the name plate
space blank and depends upon the clairvoyance of
mailmen), he in truth lives there because he cannot
afford to leave. He was rich just once in his life, and
that was in Russia, in 1964, a thaw or so ago.

Russia, in those days, like everywhere else, was a
slightly more innocent place. Khrushchev, freshly
deposed, had left an atmosphere, almost comical, of
warmth, of a certain fitful openness, of inscrutable
experiment and oblique possibility. There seemed
no overweening reason why Russia and America,
those lovable paranoid giants, could not happily
share a globe so big and blue; there certainly seemed
no reason why Henry Bech, the recherché but ami-
able novelist, artistically blocked but socially fluent,
should not be flown into Moscow at the expense of
our State Department for a month of that mostly
imaginary activity termed "cultural exchange." En-

tering the Aeroflot plane at Le Bourget, Bech
thought it smelled like his uncles' backrooms in
Williamsburg, of swaddled body heat and proxi-
mate potatoes, boiling.* The impression lingered all
month; Russia seemed Jewish to him, and of course
he seemed Jewish to Russia. He never knew how
much of the tenderness and hospitality he met re-
lated to his race. His contact man at the American
Embassy—a prissy, doleful ex-basketball-player from
Wisconsin, with the all-star name of "Skip" Reynolds,
—assured him that two out of every three Soviet
intellectuals had suppressed a Jew in their ancestry;
and once Bech did find himself in a Moscow apartment whose bookcases were lined with photographs
(of Kafka, Einstein, Freud, Wittgenstein) pointedly
evoking the glory of pre-Hitlerian *Judenkultur*. His
hosts, both man and wife, were professional translators, and the apartment was bewilderingly full of
kin, including a doe-eyed young hydraulics engineer
and a grandmother who had been a dentist with
the Red Army, and whose dental chair dominated
the parlor. For a whole long toasty evening, Jewishness, perhaps also pointedly, was not mentioned.
The subject was one Bech was happy to ignore. His
own writing had sought to reach out from the ghetto
of his heart toward the wider expanses across the
Hudson; the artistic triumph of American Jewry
lay, he thought, not in the novels of the fifties but in
the movies of the thirties, those gargantuan, crass
contraptions whereby Jewish brains projected Gen-

* See Appendix A, section I.

tile stars upon a Gentile nation and out of their own immigrant joy gave a formless land dreams and even a kind of conscience. The reservoir of faith, in 1964, was just going dry; through depression and world convulsion the country had been sustained by the *arriviste* patriotism of Louis B. Mayer and the brothers Warner. To Bech, it was one of history's great love stories, the mutually profitable romance between Jewish Hollywood and bohunk America, conducted almost entirely in the dark, a tapping of fervent messages through the wall of the San Gabriel Range; and his favorite Jewish writer was the one who turned his back on his three beautiful Brooklyn novels and went into the desert to write scripts for Doris Day. This may be, except for graduate students, neither here nor there. There, in Russia five years ago, when Cuba had been taken out of the oven to cool and Vietnam was still coming to a simmer, Bech did find a quality of life—impoverished yet ceremonial, shabby yet ornate, sentimental, embattled, and avuncular—reminiscent of his neglected Jewish past. Virtue, in Russia as in his childhood, seemed something that arose from men, like a comforting body odor, rather than something from above, that impaled the struggling soul like a moth on a pin. He stepped from the Aeroflot plane, with its notably hefty stewardesses, into an atmosphere of generosity. They met him with arms heaped with cold roses. On the first afternoon, the Writers' Union gave him as expense money a stack of ruble notes, pink and lilac Lenin and powder-blue Spasskaya

Tower. In the following month, in the guise of "royalties" (in honor of his coming they had translated
Travel Light, and several of his *Commentary* essays
["M-G-M and the U.S.A."; "The Moth on the Pin";
"Daniel Fuchs: An Appreciation"] had appeared in
I Nostrannaya Literatura, but since no copyright
agreements pertained the royalties were arbitrarily
calculated, like showers of manna), more rubles
were given to him, so that by the week of his departure Bech had accumulated over fourteen hundred rubles—by the official exchange rate, fifteen
hundred and forty dollars. There was nothing to
spend it on. All his hotels, his plane fares, his meals
were paid for. He was a guest of the Soviet state.
From morning to night he was never alone. That
first afternoon, he had also been given, along with
the rubles, a companion, a translator-escort: Ekaterina Alexandrovna Ryleyeva. She was a notably thin
red-headed woman with a flat chest and paper-
colored skin and a translucent wart above her left
nostril. He grew to call her Kate.

"Kate," he said, displaying his rubles in two fist-
fuls, letting some drift to the floor, "I have robbed
the proletariat. What can I do with my filthy loot?"
He had developed, in this long time in which she
was always with him, a clowning super-American
manner that disguised all complaints as "acts." In
response, she had strengthened her original pose—
of schoolteacherish patience, with ageless peasant roots. Her normal occupation was translating
English-language science fiction into Ukrainian, and

he imagined this month with him was relatively a
holiday. She had a mother, and late at night, after
accompanying him to a morning-brandy session with
the editors of *Yunost*, to lunch at the Writers' Union
with its shark-mouthed chairman,* to Dostoevski's
childhood home (next to a madhouse, and enshrin-
ing some agonized crosshatched manuscripts and a
pair of oval tin spectacles, tiny, as if fashioned for
a dormouse), a museum of folk art, an endless
restaurant meal, and a night of ballet, Ekaterina
would bring Bech to his hotel lobby, put a babushka
over her bushy orange hair, and head into a blizzard
toward this ailing mother. Bech wondered about
Kate's sex life. Skip Reynolds solemnly told him that
personal life in Russia was inscrutable. He also told
Bech that Kate was undoubtedly a Party spy. Bech
was touched, and wondered what in him would be
worth spying out. From infancy on we all are spies;
the shame is not this but that the secrets to be discovered are so paltry and few. Ekaterina was perhaps as old as forty, which could just give her a
lover killed in the war. Was this the secret of her
vigil, the endless paper-colored hours she spent by
his side? She was always translating for him, and
this added to her neutrality and transparence. He,
too, had never been married, and imagined that this
was what marriage was like.

She answered, "Henry"—she usually touched his
arm, saying his name, and it never ceased to thrill
him a little, the way the "H" became a breathy gut-

* See Appendix A, section II.

tural sound between "G" and "K"—"you must not joke. This is your money. You earned it by the sweat of your brain. All over Soviet Union committees of people sit in discussion over *Travel Light*, its wonderful qualities. The printing of one hundred thousand copies has gone *poof!* in the bookstores." The comic-strip colors of science fiction tinted her idiom unexpectedly.

"Poof!" Bech said, and scattered the money above his head; before the last bill stopped fluttering, they both stooped to retrieve the rubles from the rich red carpet. They were in his room at the Sovietskaya, the hotel for Party bigwigs and important visitors; all the suites were furnished in high czarist style: chandeliers, wax fruit, and brass bears.

"We have banks here," Kate said shyly, reaching under the satin sofa, "as in the capitalist countries. They pay interest, you could deposit your money in such a bank. It would be here, enlarged, when you returned. You would have a numbered bankbook."

"What?" said Bech. "And help support the Socialist state? When you are already years ahead of us in the space race? I would be adding thrust to your rockets."

They stood up, both a little breathless from exertion, betraying their age. The tip of her nose was pink. She passed the remainder of his fortune into his hands; her silence seemed embarrassed.

"Besides," Bech said, "when would I ever return?"
She offered, "Perhaps in a space-warp?"
Her shyness, her pink nose and carroty hair,

19

her embarrassment were becoming oppressive. He brusquely waved his arms. "No, Kate, we must spend it! Spend, spend. It's the Keynesian way. We will make Mother Russia a consumer society."

From the very still, slightly tipped way she was standing, Bech, bothered by "space-warp," received a haunted impression—that she was locked into a colorless other dimension from which only the pink tip of her nose emerged. "Is not so simple," she ominously pronounced.

For one thing, time was running out. Bobochka and Myshkin, the two Writers' Union officials in charge of Bech's itinerary, had crowded the end of his schedule with compulsory cultural events. Fortified by relatively leisured weeks in Kazakhstan and the Caucasus,* Bech was deemed fit to endure a marathon of war movies (the hero of one of them had lost his Communist Party member's card, which was worse than losing your driver's license; and in another a young soldier hitched rides in a maze of trains only to turn around at the end ["See, Henry," Kate whispered to him, "now he is home, that is his mother, what a good face, so much suffering, now they kiss, now he must leave, oh—" and Kate was crying too much to translate further]) and museums and shrines and brandy with various writers who uniformly adored Gemingway. November was turning bitter, the Christmassy lights celebrating

* See Appendix A, section III.

the Revolution had been taken down, Kate as they
hurried from appointment to appointment had developed a sniffle. She constantly patted her nose with
a handkerchief. Bech felt a guilty pang, sending her
off into the cold toward her mother before he ascended to his luxurious hotel room, with its par-
queted foyer stacked with gift books and its alabaster
bathroom and its great brocaded double bed. He
would drink from a gift bottle of Georgian brandy
and stand by the window, looking down on the
golden windows of an apartment building where
young Russians were Twisting to Voice of America
tapes. Chubby Checker's chicken-plucker's voice carried distinctly across the crevasse of sub-arctic
night. In an adjoining window, a couple courteously
granted isolation by the others was making love; he
could see knees and hands and then a rhythmically
kicking ankle. To relieve the pressure, Bech would
sit down with his brandy and write to distant women
boozy reminiscent letters that in the morning would
be handed solemnly to the ex-basketball-player, to
be sent out of Russia via diplomatic pouch.* Reynolds, himself something of a spy, was with them
whenever Bech spoke to a group, as of translators
(when asked who was America's best living writer,
Bech said Nabokov, and there was quite a silence
before the next question) or of students (whom he
assured that Yevtushenko's *Precocious Autobiogra-
phy* was a salubrious and patriotic work that instead
of being banned should be distributed free to Soviet

* See Appendix A, section IV.

schoolchildren). "Did I put my foot in it?" Bech
would ask anxiously afterward—another "act."

The American's careful mouth twitched. "It's good
for them. Shock therapy."

"You were charming," Ekaterina Alexandrovna always said loyally, jealously interposing herself, and
squeezing Bech's arm. She could not imagine that
Bech did not, like herself, loathe all officials. She
would not have believed that Bech approached this
one with an intellectual's reverence for the athlete,
and that they exchanged in private not anti-Kremlin
poison but literary gossip and pro football scores,
love letters and old copies of *Time*. Now, in her
campaign to keep them apart, Kate had been given
another weapon. She squeezed his arm smugly and
said, "We have an hour. We must rush off and *shop*."

For the other thing, there was not much to buy.
To begin, he would need an extra suitcase. He and
Ekaterina, in their chauffeured Zil, drove to what
seemed to Bech a far suburb, past flickerings of birch
forest, to sections of new housing, perforated ware-
houses the color of wet cement. Here they found
a vast store, vast though each salesgirl ruled as a
petty tyrant over her domain of shelves. There was
a puzzling duplication of suitcase sections; each displayed the same squarish mountain of dark cardboard boxes, and each pouting princess responded
with negative insouciance to Ekaterina's quest for a
leather suitcase. "I know there have been some," she
told Bech.

"It doesn't matter," he said. "I want a cardboard

one. I love the metal studs and the little chocolate handle."

"You have fun with me," she said. "I know what you have in the West. I have been to Science-Fiction Writers' Congress in Vienna. This great store, and not one leather suitcase. It is a disgrace upon the people. But come, I know another store." They went back into the Zil, which smelled like a cloakroom, and in whose swaying stuffy depths Bech felt squeamish and chastened, having often been sent to the cloakroom as a child at P.S. 87, on West Seventy-seventh Street and Amsterdam Avenue. A dozen stuffy miles and three more stores failed to produce a leather suitcase; at last Kate permitted him to buy a paper one—the biggest, with gay plaid sides, and as long as an oboe. To console her, he also bought an astrakhan hat. It was not flattering (when he put it on, the haughty salesgirl laughed aloud) and did not cover his ears, which were cold, but it had the advantage of costing fifty-four rubles. "Only a *boyar*," said Kate, excited to flirtation by his purchase, "would wear such a wow of a hat."

"I look like an Armenian in it," Bech said. Humiliations never come singly. On the street, with his suitcase and hat, Bech was stopped by a man who wanted to buy his overcoat. Kate translated and then scolded. During what Bech took to be a lengthy threat to call the police, the offender, a morose red-nosed man costumed like a New York chestnut vender, stared stubbornly at the sidewalk by their feet.

As they moved away, he said in soft English to Bech, "Your shoes. I give forty rubles."

Bech pulled out his wallet and said, "*Nyet, nyet.* For your shoes I give fifty."

Kate with a squawk flew between them and swept Bech away. She told him in tears, "Had the authorities witnessed that scene we would all be put in jail, biff, bang."

Bech had never seen her cry in daylight—only in the dark of projection rooms. He climbed into the Zil feeling especially sick and guilty. They were late for their luncheon, with a cherubic museum director and his hatchet-faced staff. In the course of their tour through the museum, Bech tried to cheer her up with praise of Socialist realism. "Look at that turbine. Nobody in America can paint a turbine like that. Not since the thirties. Every part so distinct you could rebuild one from it, yet the whole thing romantic as a sunset. Mimesis—you can't beat it." He was honestly fond of these huge posterish oils; they reminded him of magazine illustrations from his adolescence.

Kate would not be cheered. "It is stupid stuff," she said. "We have had no painters since Rublyov. You treat my country as a picnic." Sometimes her English had a weird precision. "It is not as if there is no talent. We are great, there are millions. The young are burning up with talent, it is annihilating them." She pronounced it *anneeheel*—a word she had met only in print, connected with ray guns.

"Kate, I *mean* it," Bech insisted, hopelessly in the

wrong, as with a third-grade teacher, yet also subject to another pressure, that of a woman taking
sensual pleasure in refusing to be consoled. "I'm telling you, there is artistic passion here. This bicycle.
Beautiful impressionism. No spokes. The French
paint apples, the Russians paint bicycles."

The parallel came out awry, unkind. Grimly patting her pink nostrils, Ekaterina passed into the next
room. "Once," she informed him, "this room held
entirely pictures of *him*. At least that is no more."

Bech did not need to ask who *he* was. The unde-
fined pronoun had a constant value. In Georgia Bech
had been shown a tombstone for a person described
simply as Mother.

The next day, between lunch with Voznesensky
and dinner with Yevtushenko (who both flatteringly
seemed to concede to him a hemispheric celebrity
equivalent to their own, and who feigned enchant-
ment when he tried to explain his peculiar status,
as not a lion, with a lion's confining burden of sym-
bolic portent, but as a graying, furtively stylish rat
indifferently permitted to gnaw and roam behind
the wainscoting of a firetrap about to be demolished
anyway), he and Kate and the impassive chauffeur
managed to buy three amber necklaces and four
wooden toys and two very thin wristwatches. The
amber seemed homely to Bech—melted butter re-
frozen—but Kate was proud of it. The wristwatches
he suspected would soon stop; they were perilously
thin. The toys—segmented Kremlins, carved bears
chopping wood—were good, but the only children

he knew were his sister's in Cincinnati, and the youngest was nine. The Ukrainian needlework that Ekaterina hopefully pushed at him his imagination could not impose on any woman he knew, not even his mother; since his "success," she had her hair done once a week and wore her hems just above the knee. Back in his hotel room, in the ten minutes before an all-Shostakovich concert, while Kate sniffled and sloshed in the bathroom (how could such a skinny woman be displacing all that water?), Bech counted his rubles. He had spent only a hundred and thirty-seven. That left one thousand two hundred and eighty-three, plus the odd kopecks. His heart sank; it was hopeless. Ekaterina emerged from the bathroom with a strange, bruised stare. Little burnt traces, traces of ashen tears, lingered about her eyes, which were by nature a washed-out blue. She had been trying to put on eye makeup, and had kept washing it off. Trying to be a rich man's wife. She looked blank and wounded. Bech took her arm; they hurried downstairs like criminals on the run.

The next day was his last full day in Russia. All month he had wanted to visit Tolstoy's estate, and the trip had been postponed until now. Since Yasnaya Polyana was four hours from Moscow, he and Kate left early in the morning and returned in the dark. After miles of sleepy silence, she asked, "Henry, what did you like?"

"I liked the way he wrote *War and Peace* in the

cellar, *Anna Karenina* on the first floor, and *Resur-
rection* upstairs. Do you think he's writing a fourth
novel in Heaven?"

This reply, taken from a little *Commentary* article
he was writing in his head (and would never write
on paper), somehow renewed her silence. When she
at last spoke, her voice was shy. "As a Jew, you
believe?"

His laugh had an ambushed quality he tried to
translate, with a shy guffaw at the end, into self-
deprecation. "Jews don't go in much for Paradise,"
he said. "That's something you Christians cooked
up."

"We are not Christians."

"Kate, you are saints. You are a land of monks
and your government is a constant penance." From
the same unwritten article—tentatively titled
"God's Ghost in Moscow." He went on, with Hollywood, Martin Buber, and his uncles all vaguely
smiling in his mind, "I think the Jewish feeling is
that wherever they happen to be, it's rather para-
disiacal, because they're there."

"You have found it so here?"

"Very much. This must be the only country in the
world you can be homesick for while you're still in
it. Russia is one big case of homesickness."

Perhaps Kate found this ground dangerous, for she
returned to earlier terrain. "It is strange," she said,
"of the books I translate, how much there is to do
with supernature. Immaterial creatures like angels,
ideal societies composed of spirits, speeds that ex-

ceed that of light, reversals of time—all impossible, and perhaps not. In a way it is terrible, to look up at the sky, on one of our clear nights of burning cold, at the sky of stars, and think of creatures alive in it."

"Like termites in the ceiling." Falling so short of the grandeur Kate might have had a right to expect from him, his simile went unanswered. The car swayed, dark gingerbread villages swooped by, the back of the driver's head was motionless. Bech idly hummed a bit of "Midnight in Moscow," whose literal title, he had discovered, was "Twilit Evenings in the Moscow Suburbs." He said, "I also liked the way Upton Sinclair was in his bookcase, and how his house felt like a farmhouse instead of a mansion, and his grave."

"So super a grave."

"Very graceful, for a man who fought death so hard." It had been an unmarked oval of earth, rimmed green with frozen turf, at the end of a road in a birchwood where night was sifting in. It had been here that Tolstoy's brother had told him to search for the little green stick that would end war and human suffering. Because her importunate silence had begun to nag unbearably, Bech told Kate, "That's what I should do with my rubles. Buy Tolstoy a tombstone. With a neon arrow."

"Oh those rubles!" she exclaimed. "You persecute me with those rubles. We have shopped more in one week than I shop in one year. Material things do not interest me, Henry. In the war we all learned the value of material things. There is no value but what you hold within yourself."

"O.K., I'll swallow them."

"Always the joke. I have one more desperate idea. In New York, you have women for friends?"

Her voice had gone shy, as when broaching Jewishness; she was asking him if he were a homosexual. How little, after a month, these two knew each other! "Yes. I have *only* women for friends."

"Then perhaps we could buy them some furs. Not a coat, the style would be wrong. But fur we have, not leather suitcases, no, you are right to mock us, but furs, the world's best, and dear enough for even a man so rich as you. I have often argued with Bobochka, he says authors should be poor for the suffering, it is how capitalist countries do it; and now I see he is right."

Astounded by this tirade, delivered with a switching head so that her mole now and then darted into translucence—for they had reached Moscow's outskirts, and street lamps—Bech could only say, "Kate, you've never read my books. They're *all* about women."

"Yes," she said, "but coldly observed. As if extraterrestrial life."

To be brief (I saw you, in the back row, glancing at your wristwatch, and don't think that glance will sweeten your term grade), fur it was. The next morning, in a scrambled hour before the ride to the airport,

Bech and Ekaterina went to a shop on Gorky Street where a diffident Mongolian beauty laid pelt after pelt into his hands. The less unsuccessful of his uncles had been for a time a furrier, and after this gap of decades Bech again greeted the frosty luxuriance of silver fox, the more tender and playful and amorous amplitude of red fox, mink with its ugly mahogany assurance, svelte otter, imperial ermine tail-tipped in black like a writing plume. Each pelt, its soft tingling mass condensing acres of Siberia, cost several hundred rubles. Bech bought for his mother two mink still wearing their dried snarls, and two silver fox for his present mistress, Norma Latchett, to trim a coat collar in (her firm white Saxon chin *drowned* in fur, is how he pictured it), and some ermine as a joke for his house-slave sister in Cincinnati, and a sumptuous red fox for a woman he had yet to meet. The Mongolian salesgirl, magnificently unimpressed, added it up to over twelve hundred rubles and wrapped the furs in brown paper like fish. He paid her with a salad of pastel notes and was clean. Bech had not been so exhilarated, so aërated by prosperity, since he sold his first short story—in 1943, about boot camp, to *Liberty,* for a hundred and fifty dollars. It had been humorous, a New York Jew floundering among Southerners, and is omitted from most bibliographies.*

He and Ekaterina rushed back to the Sovietskaya and completed his packing. He tried to forget the gift books stacked in the foyer, but she insisted he

* See Appendix B.

take them. They crammed them into his new suitcase, with the furs, the amber, the wristwatches, the
infuriatingly knobby and bulky wooden toys. When
they were done, the suitcase bulged, leaked fur, and
weighed more than his two others combined. Bech
looked his last at the chandelier and the empty
brandy bottle, the lovesick window and the bugged
walls, and staggered out the door. Kate followed
with a book and a sock she had found beneath the
bed.

Everyone was at the airport to see him off—Bobochka with his silver teeth, Myshkin with his glass
eye, the rangy American with his air of lugubrious
caution. Bech shook Skip Reynolds's hand goodbye
and abrasively kissed the two Russian men on the
cheek. He went to kiss Ekaterina on the cheek, but
she turned her face so that her mouth met his and he
realized, horrified, that he should have slept with
her. He had been expected to. From the complacent
tiptoe smiles of Bobochka and Myshkin, they assumed he had. She had been provided to him for
that purpose. He was a guest of the state. "Oh, Kate,
forgive me; of course," he said, but so stumblingly
she seemed not to have understood him. Her kiss
had been colorless but moist and good, like a boiled
potato.

Then, somehow, suddenly, he was late, there was
panic. His suitcases were not yet in the airplane. A
brute in blue seized the two manageable ones and
left him to carry the paper one himself. As he staggered across the runway, it burst. One catch simply

tore loose at the staples, and the other sympathet-
ically let go. The books and toys spilled; the fur began to blow down the concrete, pelts looping and
shimmering as if again alive. Kate broke past the
gate guard and helped him catch them; together they
scooped all the loot back in the suitcase, but for a
dozen fluttering books. They were heavy and slick,
in the Cyrillic alphabet, like high-school yearbooks
upside down. One of the watches had cracked its
face. Kate was sobbing and shivering in excitement;
a bitter wind was blowing streaks of grit and snow
out of the coming long winter. "Genry, the books!"
she said, needing to shout. "You must have them!
They are souvenirs!"

"Mail them!" Bech thundered, and ran with the
terrible suitcase under his arm, fearful of being bur-
dened with more responsibilities. Also, though in
some ways a man of our time, he has a morbid fear
of missing airplanes, and of being dropped from the
tail-end lavatory.

Though this was five years ago, the books have not
yet arrived in the mail. Perhaps Ekaterina Alexandrovna kept them, as souvenirs. Perhaps they were
caught in the cultural freeze-up that followed Bech's
visit, and were buried in a blizzard. Perhaps they
arrived in the lobby of his apartment building, and
were pilfered by an émigré vandal. Or perhaps(you
may close your notebooks) the mailman is not clair-
voyant after all.

Bech in Rumania;

or, The Rumanian Chauffeur

DEPLANING IN BUCHAREST wearing an astrakhan hat purchased in Moscow, Bech was not recognized by the United States Embassy personnel sent to greet him, and, rather than identify himself, sat sullenly on a bench, glowering like a Soviet machinery importer, while these young men ran back and forth conversing with each other in dismayed English and shouting at the customs officials in what Bech took to be pidgin Rumanian. At last, one of these young men, the smallest and cleverest, Princeton '51 or so, noticing the rounded toes of Bech's American shoes, ventured suspiciously, "I beg your pardon, *pazhalusta*, but are you—?"

"Could be," Bech said. After five weeks of consorting with Communists, he felt himself increasingly tempted to evade, confuse, and mock his fellow Americans. Further, after attuning himself to the platitudinous jog of translatorese, he found rapid English idiom exhausting. So it was with some relief that he passed, in the next hours, from the conspiratorial company of his compatriots into the care of a monarchial Rumanian hotel and a smiling Party underling called Athanase Petrescu.

Petrescu, whose oval face was adorned by constant sunglasses and several round sticking plasters placed upon a fresh blue shave, had translated into Rumanian *Typee*, *Pierre*, *Life on the Mississippi*, *Sister Carrie*, *Winesburg, Ohio*, *Across the River and Into the Trees*, and *On the Road*. He knew Bech's work well and said, "Although it was *Travel Light* that made your name illustrious, yet in my heart I detect a very soft spot for *Brother Pig*, which your critics did not so much applaud."

Bech recognized in Petrescu, behind the blue jaw and sinister glasses, a man humbly in love with books, a fool for literature. As, that afternoon, they strolled through a dreamlike Bucharest park containing bronze busts of Goethe and Pushkin and Victor Hugo, beside a lake wherein the greenish sunset was coated with silver, the translator talked excitedly of a dozen things, sharing thoughts he had not been able to share while descending, alone at his desk, into the luminous abysses and profound crudities of American literature. "With Hemingway, the difficulty of translating—and I speak to an extent of Anderson also—is to prevent the simplicity from seeming simpleminded. For we do not have here such a tradition of belle-lettrist fancifulness against which the style of Hemingway was a rebel. Do you follow the difficulty?"

"Yes. How did you get around it?"

Petrescu did not seem to understand. "Get around, how? Circumvent?"

"How did you translate the simple language without seeming simple-minded?"

"Oh. By being extremely subtle."

"Oh. I should tell you, some people in my country think Hemingway *was* simple-minded. It is actively debated."

Petrescu absorbed this with a nod, and said, "I know for a fact, his Italian is not always correct."

When Bech got back to his hotel—situated on a square rimmed with buildings made, it seemed, of dusty pink candy—a message had been left for him to call Phillips at the U.S. Embassy. Phillips was Princeton '51. He asked, "What have they got mapped out for you?"

Bech's schedule had hardly been discussed. "Petrescu mentioned a production of *Desire Under the Elms* I might see. And he wants to take me to Braşov. Where is Braşov?"

"In Transylvania, way the hell off. It's where Dracula hung out. Listen, can we talk frankly?"

"We can try."

"I know damn well this line is bugged, but here goes. This country is hot. Anti-Socialism is busting out all over. My inkling is they want to get you out of Bucharest, away from all the liberal writers who are dying to meet you."

"Are you sure they're not dying to meet Arthur Miller?"

"Kidding aside, Bech, there's a lot of ferment in this country, and we want to plug you in. Now, when are you meeting Taru?"

"Knock knock. Taru. Taru Who?"

"Jesus, he's the head of the Writers' Union—hasn't Petrescu even set up an appointment? Boy, they're putting you right around the old mulberry bush. I gave Petrescu a list of writers for you to latch on to. Suppose I call him and wave the big stick and ring you back. Got it?"

"Got it, tiger." Bech hung up sadly; one of the reasons he had accepted the State Department's invitation was that he thought it would be an escape from agents.

Within ten minutes his phone rasped, in that dead rattly way it has behind the Iron Curtain, and it was Phillips, breathless, victorious. "Congratulate me," he said. "I've been making like a thug and got *their* thugs to give you an appointment with Taru tonight."

"This very night?"

Phillips sounded hurt. "You're only here four nights, you know. Petrescu will pick you up. His excuse was he thought you might want some rest."

"He's extremely subtle."

"What was that?"

"Never mind, *pazhalusta.*"

Petrescu came for Bech in a black car driven by a hunched silhouette. The Writers' Union was housed on the other side of town, in a kind of castle, a turreted mansion with a flaring stone staircase and an oak-vaulted library whose shelves were twenty feet high and solid with leather spines. The stairs and chambers seemed deserted. Petrescu tapped on a tall paneled door of blackish oak, strap-hinged in the sombre Spanish style. The door soundlessly opened, revealing a narrow high room hung with tapestries, pale brown and blue, whose subject involved masses of attenuated soldiery unfathomably engaged. Behind a huge polished desk quite bare of furnishings sat an immaculate miniature man with a pink face and hair as white as a dandelion poll. His rosy hands, perfectly finished down to each fingernail, were folded on the shiny desk, reflected like water flowers; and his face wore a smiling expression that was also, in each neat crease, beyond improvement. This was Taru.

He spoke with magical suddenness, like a music box. Petrescu translated his words to Bech as, "You are a literary man. Do you know the works of our Mihail Sadoveanu, of our noble Mihai Beniuc, or perhaps that most wonderful spokesman for the people, Tudor Arghezi?"

Bech said, "No, I'm afraid the only Rumanian writer I know at all is Ionesco."

The exquisite white-haired man nodded eagerly and emitted a length of tinkling sounds that was translated to Bech as simply "And who is he?"

Petrescu, who certainly knew all about Ionesco, stared at Bech with blank expectance. Even in this innermost sanctum he had kept his sunglasses on.

Bech said, irritated, "A playwright. Lives in Paris. Theatre of the Absurd. Wrote *Rhinoceros*," and he crooked a forefinger beside his heavy Jewish nose, to represent a horn.

Taru emitted a dainty sneeze of laughter. Petrescu translated, listened, and told Bech, "He is very sorry he has not heard of this man. Western books are a luxury here, so we are not able to follow each new nihilist movement. Comrade Taru asks what you plan to do while in the People's Republic of Rumania."

"I am told," Bech said, "that there are some writers interested in exchanging ideas with an American colleague. I believe my embassy has suggested a list to you."

The musical voice went on and on. Petrescu listened with a cocked ear and relayed, "Comrade Taru sincerely wishes that this may be the case and regrets that, because of the lateness of the hour and the haste of this meeting urged by your embassy, no secretaries are present to locate this list. He furthermore regrets that at this time of the year so many of our fine writers are bathing at the Black Sea. However, he points out that there is an excellent production of *Desire Under the Elms* in Bucharest, and that our Carpathian city of Braşov is indeed worthy of a visit. Comrade Taru himself retains many pleasant youthful memories concerning Braşov."

Taru rose to his feet—an intensely dramatic event within the reduced scale he had established around himself. He spoke, thumped his small square chest resoundingly, spoke again, and smiled. Petrescu said,

"He wishes you to know that in his youth he published many books of poetry, both epic and lyric in manner. He adds, 'A fire ignited here' "—and here Petrescu struck his own chest in flaccid mimicry—" 'can never be quenched.' "

Bech stood and responded, "In my country we also ignite fires *here*." He touched his head. His remark was not translated and, after an efflorescent display of courtesy from the brilliant-haired little man, Bech and Petrescu made their way through the empty mansion down to the waiting car, which drove them, rather jerkily, back to the hotel.

"And how did you like Mr. Taru?" Petrescu asked on the way.

"He's a doll," Bech said.

"You mean—a puppet?"

Bech turned curiously but saw nothing in Petrescu's face that betrayed more than a puzzlement over meaning. Bech said, "I'm sure you have a better eye for the strings than I do."

Since neither had eaten, they dined together at the hotel; they discussed Faulkner and Hawthorne while waiters brought them soup and veal a continent removed from the cabbagy cuisine of Russia. A lithe young woman on awkwardly high heels stalked among the tables singing popular songs from Italy and France. The trailing microphone wire now and then became entangled in her feet, and Bech admired the sly savagery with which she would, while not altering an iota her enameled smile, kick herself free. Bech had been a long time without a woman. He looked forward to three more nights sitting at this table, surrounded by traveling salesmen from East Germany and Hungary, feasting on the sight of this lithe chanteuse. Though her motions were angular and her smile was inflexible, her high round bosom looked soft as a soufflé.

But tomorrow, Petrescu explained, smiling sweetly beneath his sad-eyed sunglasses, they would go to Braşov.

Bech knew little about Rumania. From his official briefing he knew it was "a Latin island in a Slavic sea," that during World War II its anti-Semitism had been the most ferocious in Europe, that now it was seeking economic independence of the Soviet bloc. The ferocity especially interested him, since of the many human conditions it was his business to imagine, murderousness was among the more difficult. He was a Jew. Though he could be irritable and even vengeful, obstinate savagery was excluded from his budget of emotions.

Petrescu met him in the hotel lobby at nine and, taking his suitcase from his hand, led him to the hired car. By daylight, the chauffeur was a short man the color of ashes—white ash for the face, gray cigarette ash for his close-trimmed smudge of a mustache, and the darker residue of a tougher substance for his eyes and hair. His manner was nervous and remote and fussy; Bech's impression was of a stupidity so severe that the mind is tensed to sustain the simplest tasks. As they drove from the city, the driver constantly tapped his horn to warn pedestrians and cyclists of his approach. They passed the prewar stucco suburbs, suggestive of southern California; the postwar Moscow-style apartment buildings, rectilinear and airless; the heretical all-glass exposition hall the Rumanians had built to celebrate twenty years of industrial progress under Socialism. It was shaped like a huge sailor's cap, and before it stood a tall Brancusi column cast in aluminum.

"Brancusi," Bech said. "I didn't know you acknowledged him."

"Oh, much," Petrescu said. "His village is a shrine. I can show you many early works in our national museum."

"And Ionesco? Is he really a non-person?"

Petrescu smiled. "The eminent head of our Writers' Union," he said, "makes little jokes. He is known here but not much produced as yet. Students in their rooms perhaps read aloud a play like *The Singer Devoid of Hair.*"

Bech was distracted from the conversation by the driver's incessant mutter of tooting. They were in the country now, driving along a straight, slightly rising road lined with trees whose trunks were painted white. On the shoulder of the road walked bundle-shaped old women carrying knotted bundles, little boys tapping donkeys forward, men in French-blue work clothes sauntering empty-handed. At all of them the driver sounded his horn. His stubby, gray-nailed hand fluttered on the contact rim, producing an agitated stammer beginning perhaps a hundred yards in advance and continuing until the person, who usually moved only to turn and scowl, had been passed. Since the road was well traveled, the noise was practically uninterrupted, and after the first half hour nagged Bech like a toothache. He asked Petrescu, "Must he do that?"

"Oh, yes. He is a conscientious man."

"What good does it do?"

Petrescu, who had been developing an exciting thought on Mark Twain's infatuation with the apparatus of capitalism, which had undermined his bucolic genius, indulgently explained, "The bureau from which we hire cars provides the driver. They have been precisely trained for this profession."

Bech realized that Petrescu himself did not drive. He reposed in the oblivious trust of an airplane passenger, legs crossed, sunglasses in place, issuing smoother and smoother phrases, while Bech leaned forward anxiously, braking on the empty floor, twitching a wheel that was not there, trying to wrench the car's control away from this atrociously unrhythmic and brutal driver. When they went through a village, the driver would speed up and intensify the mutter of his honking; clusters of peasants and geese exploded in disbelief, and Bech felt as if gears, the gears that space and engage the mind, were clashing. As they ascended into the mountains, the driver demonstrated his technique with curves: he approached each like an enemy, accelerating, and at the last moment stepped on the brake as if crushing a snake underfoot. In the jerking and swaying, Petrescu grew pale. His blue jaw acquired a moist sheen and issued phrases less smoothly. Bech said to him, "This driver should be locked up. He is sick and dangerous."

"No, no, he is a good man. These roads, they are difficult."

"At least please ask him to stop twiddling the horn. It's torture."

Petrescu's eyebrows arched, but he leaned forward and spoke in Rumanian.

The driver answered; the language clattered in his mouth, though his voice was soft.

Petrescu told Bech, "He says it is a safety precaution."

"Oh, for Christ's sake!"

Petrescu was truly puzzled. He asked, "In the States, you drive your own car?"

"Of course, everybody does," Bech said, and then worried that he had hurt the feelings of this Socialist, who must submit to the aristocratic discomfort of being driven. For the remainder of the trip, he held silent about the driver. The muddy lowland fields with Mediterranean farmhouses had yielded to fir-dark hills bearing Germanic chalets. At the highest point, the old boundary of Austria-Hungary, fresh snow had fallen, and the car, pressed ruthlessly through the ruts, brushed within inches of some children dragging sleds. It was a short downhill distance from there to Braşov. They stopped before a newly built pistachio hotel. The jarring ride had left

Bech with a headache. Petrescu stepped carefully from the car, licking his lips; the tip of his tongue showed purple in his drained face. The chauffeur, as composed as raked ashes no touch of wind has stirred, changed out of his gray driving coat, checked the oil and water, and removed his lunch from the trunk. Bech examined him for some sign of satisfaction, some betraying trace of malice, but there was nothing. His eyes were living smudges, and his mouth was the mouth of the boy in the class who, being neither strong nor intelligent, has developed insignificance into a positive character trait that does him some credit. He glanced at Bech without expression; yet Bech wondered if the man did not understand English a little.

In Braşov the American writer and his escort passed the time in harmless sightseeing. The local museum contained peasant costumes. The local castle contained armor. The Lutheran cathedral was surprising; Gothic lines and scale had been wedded to clear glass and an austerity of decoration, noble and mournful, that left one, Bech felt, much too alone with God. He felt the Reformation here as a desolating wind, four hundred years ago. From the hotel roof, the view looked sepia, and there was an empty swimming pool, and wet snow on the lacy metal chairs. Petrescu shivered and went down to his room. Bech changed neckties and went down to the bar. Champagne music bubbled from the walls.

The bartender understood what a Martini was, though he used equal parts of gin and vermouth. The clientele was young, and many spoke Hungarian, for Transylvania had been taken from Hungary after the war. One plausible youth, working with Bech's reluctant French, elicited from him that he was *un écrivain*, and asked for his autograph. But this turned out to be the prelude to a proposed exchange of pens, in which Bech lost a sentimentally cherished Esterbrook and gained a nameless ballpoint that wrote red. Bech wrote three and a half postcards (to his mistress, his mother, his publisher, and a half to his editor at *Commentary*) before the red pen went dry. Petrescu, who neither drank nor smoked, finally appeared. Bech said, "My hero, where have you been? I've had four Martinis and been swindled in your absence."

Petrescu was embarrassed. "I've been shaving."

"Shaving!"

"Yes, it is humiliating. I must spend each day one hour shaving, and even yet it does not look as if I have shaved, my beard is so obdurate."

"Are you putting blades in the razor?"

"Oh, yes, I buy the best and use two upon each occasion."

"This is the saddest story I've ever heard. Let me send you some decent blades when I get home."

"Please, do not. There are no blades better than the blades I use. It is merely that my beard is phenomenal."

45

"When you die," Bech said, "you can leave it to Rumanian science."

"You are ironical."

In the restaurant, there was dancing—the Tveest, the Hully Gullee, and chain formations that involved a lot of droll hopping. American dances had become here innocently birdlike. Now and then a young man, slender and with hair combed into a parrot's peak, would leap into the air and seem to hover, emitting a shrill palatal cry. The men in Rumania appeared lighter and more fanciful than the women, who moved, in their bell-skirted cocktail dresses, with a wooden stateliness perhaps inherited from their peasant grandmothers. Each girl who passed near their table was described by Petrescu, not humorously at first, as a "typical Rumanian beauty."

"And this one, with the orange lips and eyelashes?"

"A typical Rumanian beauty. The cheekbones are very classical."

"And the blonde behind her? The small plump one?"

"Also typical."

"But they are so different. Which is more typical?"

"They are equally. We are a perfect democracy." Between spates of dancing, a young chanteuse, more talented than the one in the Bucharest hotel, took the floor. She had learned, probably from free-world films, that terrible mannerism of strenuousness whereby every note, no matter how accessibly placed and how flatly attacked, is given a facial aura

of immense accomplishment. Her smile, at the close
of each number, triumphantly combined a conspiratorial twinkle, a sublime humility, and the dazed
self-congratulation of post-coital euphoria. Yet, beneath the artifice, the girl had life. Bech was
charmed by a number, in Italian, that involved
much animated pouting and finger-scolding and
placing of the fists on the hips. Petrescu explained
that the song was the plaint of a young wife whose
husband was always attending soccer matches and
never stayed home with her. Bech asked, "Is she also
a typical Rumanian beauty?"

"I think," Petrescu said, with a purr Bech had not
heard before, "she is a typical little Jewess."

The drive, late the next afternoon, back to Bucharest was worse than the one out, for it took place
partly in the dark. The chauffeur met the challenge
with increased speed and redoubled honking. In a
rare intermittence of danger, a straight road near
Ploeşti where only the oil rigs relieved the flatness,
Bech asked, "Seriously, do you not feel the insanity
in this man?" Five minutes before, the driver had
turned to the back seat and, showing even gray teeth
in a tight tic of a smile, had remarked about a dog
lying dead beside the road. Bech suspected that most
of the remark had not been translated.

Petrescu said, crossing his legs in the effete and
weary way that had begun to exasperate Bech, "No,
he is a good man, an extremely kind man, who takes
his work too seriously. In that he is like the beautiful
Jewess whom you so much admired."

"In my country," Bech said, "'Jewess' is a kind of fighting word."

"Here," Petrescu said, "it is merely descriptive. Let us talk about Herman Melville. Is it possible to you that *Pierre* is a yet greater work than *The White Whale?*"

"No, I think it is yet not so great, possibly."

"You are ironical about my English. Please excuse it. Being prone to motion sickness has discollected my thoughts."

"Our driver would discollect anybody's thoughts. Is it possible that he is the late Adolf Hitler, kept alive by Count Dracula?"

"I think not. Our people's uprising in 1944 fortunately exterminated the Fascists."

"That is fortunate. Have you ever read, speaking of Melville, *Omoo?*"

Melville, it happened, was Bech's favorite American author, in whom he felt united the strengths that were later to go the separate ways of Dreiser and James. Throughout dinner, back at the hotel, he lectured Petrescu about him. "No one," Bech said— he had ordered a full bottle of white Rumanian wine, and his tongue felt agile as a butterfly—"more courageously faced our native terror. He went for it right between its wide-set little pig eyes, and it shattered his genius like a lance." He poured himself more wine. The hotel chanteuse, who Bech now noticed had buck teeth as well as gawky legs, stalked to their table, untangled her feet from the micro-

phone wire, and favored them with a French version
of "Some Enchanted Evening."

"You do not consider," Petrescu said, "that Hawthorne also went between the eyes? And the laconic
Ambrose Bierce?"

"*Quelque soir enchanté*," the girl sang, her eyes
and teeth and earrings glittering like the facets of a
chandelier.

"Hawthorne blinked," Bech pronounced, "and
Bierce squinted."

"*Vous verrez l'étranger . . .*"

"I worry about you, Petrescu," Bech continued.
"Don't you ever have to go home? Isn't there a Frau
Petrescu, Madame, or whatever, a typical Rumanian,
never mind." Abruptly he felt steeply lonely.

In bed, when his room had stopped the gentle
swaying motion with which it had greeted his entrance, he remembered the driver, and the man's
neatly combed death-gray face seemed the face of
everything foul, stale, stupid, and uncontrollable in
the world. He had seen that tight tic of a smile before. Where? He remembered. West Eighty-sixth
Street, coming back from Riverside Park, a childhood
playmate, with whom he always argued, and was always right, and always lost. Their ugliest quarrel had
concerned comic strips, whether or not the artist—
Segar, say, who drew Popeye, or Harold Gray of
Little Orphan Annie—whether or not the artist, in
duplicating the faces from panel to panel, day after
day, traced them. Bech had maintained, obviously,
not. The other boy had insisted that some mechan-

ical process was used. Bech tried to explain that it was not such a difficult feat, that just as one's handwriting is always the same— The other boy, his face clouding, said it wasn't possible. Bech explained, what he felt so clearly, that everything was possible for human beings, with a little training and talent, that the ease and variation of each panel proved— The other face had become totally closed, with a density quite inhuman, as it steadily shook "No, no, no," and Bech, becoming frightened and furious, tried to behead the other boy with his fists, and the boy in turn pinned him and pressed his face into the bitter grits of pebble and glass that coated the cement passageway between two apartment buildings. These unswept jagged bits, a kind of city topsoil, had enlarged under his eyes, and this experience, the magnification amidst pain of those negligible mineral flecks, had formed, perhaps, a vision. At any rate, it seemed to Bech, as he skidded into sleep, that his artistic gifts had been squandered in the attempt to recapture that moment of stinging precision.

The next day was his last full day in Rumania. Petrescu took him to an art museum where, amid many ethnic posters posing as paintings, a few sketches and sculpted heads by the young Brancusi smelled like saints' bones. The two men went on to the twenty years' industrial exhibit and admired rows of brightly painted machinery—gaudy counters in some large international game. They visited shops, and everywhere Bech felt a desiccated pinkish elegance groping, out of eclipse, through the murky hardware of Sovietism, toward a rebirth of style. Yet there had been a tough and heroic naïveté in Russia that he missed here, where something shrugging and effete seemed to leave room for a vein of energetic evil. In the evening, they went to *Patima de Sub Ulmi.*

Their driver, bringing them to the very door of the theatre, pressed his car forward through bodies, up an arc of driveway crowded with pedestrians. The people caught in the headlights were astonished; Bech slammed his foot on a phantom brake and Petrescu grunted and strained backward in his seat. The driver continually tapped his horn—a demented, persistent muttering—and slowly the crowd gave way around the car. Bech and Petrescu stepped, at the door, into the humid atmosphere of a riot. As the chauffeur, his childish small-nosed profile intent, pressed his car back through the crowd to the street, fists thumped on the fenders.

Safe in the theatre lobby, Petrescu took off his sunglasses to wipe his face. His eyes were a tender bulging blue, with jaundiced whites; a scholar's tremor pulsed in his left lower lid. "You know," he confided to Bech, "that man our driver. Not all is well with him."

"Could be," Bech said.

O'Neill's starveling New England farmers were played as Russian muzhiks; they wore broad-belted coats and high black boots and kept walloping each

other on the back. Abbie Cabot had become a typical
Rumanian beauty, ten years past prime, with a
beauty spot on one cheek and artful bare arms as
supple as a swan's neck. Since their seats were in
the center of the second row, Bech had a good if
infrequent view down the front of her dress, and
thus, ignorant of when the plot would turn her his
way, he contentedly manufactured suspense for
himself. But Petrescu, his loyalty to American letters affronted beyond endurance, insisted that they
leave after the first act. "Wrong, wrong," he complained. "Even the pitchforks were wrong."

"I'll have the State Department send them an au-
thentic American pitchfork," Bech promised.

"And the girl—the girl is not like that, not a coquette. She is a religious innocent, under economic
stress."

"Well, scratch an innocent, find a coquette."

"It is your good nature to joke, but I am ashamed
you saw such a travesty. Now our driver is not here.
We are undone."

The street outside the theatre, so recently jammed,
was empty and dark. A solitary couple walked slowly
toward them. With surrealist suddenness, Petrescu
fell into the arms of the man, walloping his back, and
then kissed the calmly proffered hand of the woman.
The couple was introduced to Bech as "a most bril-
liant young writer and his notably ravishing wife."
The man, stolid and forbidding, wore rimless glasses
and a bulky checked topcoat. The woman was
scrawny; her face, potentially handsome, had been

worn to its bones by the nervous stress of intelligence. She had a cold and a command, quick but limited, of English. "Are you having a liking for this?" she asked.

Bech understood her gesture to include all Rumania. "Very much," he answered. "After Russia, it seems very civilized."

"And who isn't?" she snapped. "What are you liking most?"

Petrescu roguishly interposed, "He has a passion for night-club singers."

The wife translated this to her husband; he took his hands from his overcoat pockets and clapped them. He was wearing leather gloves, so the noise was loud on the deserted street. He spoke, and Petrescu translated, "He says we should therefore, as hosts, escort you to the most celebrated night club in Bucharest, where you will see many singers, each more glorious than the preceding."

"But," Bech said, "weren't they going somewhere? Shouldn't they go home?" It worried him that Communists never seemed to go home.

"For why?" the wife cried.

"You have a cold," Bech told her. Her eyes didn't comprehend. He touched his own nose, so much larger than hers. "*Un rhume.*"

"Poh!" she said. "Itself takes care of tomorrow."

The writer owned a car, and he drove them, with the gentleness of a pedal boat, through a maze of alleys overhung by cornices suggestive of cake frosting, of waves breaking, of seashells, lion paws, unicorn horns, and cumulus clouds. They parked across the street from a blue sign, and went into a green doorway, and down a yellow set of stairs. Music approached them from one direction and a coat-check girl in net tights from the other. It was to Bech as if he were dreaming of an American night club, giving it the strange spaciousness of dreams. The main room had been conjured out of several basements—a cave hollowed from the underside of jeweler's shops and vegetable marts. Tables were set in shadowy tiers arranged around a central square floor. Here a man with a red wig and mascaraed eyes was talking into a microphone, mincingly. Then he sang, in the voice of a choirboy castrated too late. A waiter materialized. Bech ordered Scotch, the other writer ordered vodka. The wife asked for cognac and Petrescu for mineral water. Three girls dressed as rather naked bicyclists appeared with a dwarf on a unicycle and did some unsmiling gyrations to music while he pedalled among them, tugging bows and displacing straps. "Typical Polish beauties," Petrescu explained in Bech's ear. He and the writer's wife were seated on the tier behind Bech. Two women, one a girl in her teens and the other a heavy old blonde, perhaps her mother, both dressed identically in sequined silver, did a hypnotic, languorous act with tinted pigeons, throwing them up in the air, watching them wheel through the shadows of the night club, and holding out their wrists for their return. They juggled with the pigeons, passed them between their legs, and for a climax the elderly blonde fed an aquamarine pigeon with seeds held in her mouth and fetched, one by one, onto her lips. "Czechs," Petrescu explained. The master of ceremonies reappeared in a blue wig and a toreador's jacket, and did a comic act with the dwarf, who had been fitted with papier-mâché horns. An East German girl, flaxen-haired and apple-cheeked, with the smooth columnar legs of the very young, came to the microphone dressed in a minimal parody of a cowgirl outfit and sang, in English, "Dip in the Hot of Texas" and "Allo Cindy Lou, Gootbye Hot." She pulled guns from her hips and received much pro-American applause, but Bech was on his third Scotch and needed his hands to hold cigarettes. The Rumanian writer sat at the table beside him, a carafe of vodka at his elbow, staring stolidly at the floor show. He looked like the young Theodore Roosevelt, or perhaps McGeorge Bundy. His wife leaned forward and said in Bech's ear, "Is just like home, hey? Texas is ringing bells?" He decided she was being sarcastic. A fat man in a baggy maroon tuxedo set up a long table and kept eight tin plates twirling on the ends of flexible sticks. Bech thought it was miraculous, but the man was booed. A touching black-haired girl from Bulgaria hesitantly sang three atonal folk songs into a chastened silence. Three women behind Bech began to chatter hissingly. Bech turned to rebuke them and was stunned by the size of their wristwatches, which were man-sized, as in Russia. Also, in turning he had surprised Petrescu and the writer's wife holding hands. Though it was after midnight, the custom-

ers were still coming in, and the floor show refused
to stop. The Polish girls returned dressed as ponies
and jumped through hoops the dwarf held for them.
The master of ceremonies reappeared in a striped
bathing suit and black wig and did an act with the
dwarf involving a stepladder and a bucket of water.
A black dancer from Ghana twirled firebrands in the
dark while slapping the floor with her bare feet. Four
Latvian tumblers performed on a trampoline and a
seesaw. The Czech mother and daughter came back
in different costumes, spangled gold, but performed
the identical act, the pigeons whirring, circling, returning, eating from the mother's lips. Then five Chinese girls from Outer Mongolia—

"My God," Bech said, "isn't this ever going to be
over? Don't you Communists ever get tired of having
fun?"

The writer's wife told him, "For your money, you
really gets."

Petrescu and she conferred and decided it was
time to go. One of the big wristwatches behind Bech
said two o'clock. In leaving, they had to pass
around the Chinese girls, who, each clad in a snug
beige bikini, were concealing and revealing their
bodies amid a weave of rippling colored flags. One
of the girls glanced sideways at Bech, and he blew
her a pert kiss, as if from a train window. Their yellow bodies looked fragile to him; he felt that their
bones, like the bones of birds, had evolved hollow,
to save weight. At the mouth of the cave, the effemi-
nate master of ceremonies, wearing a parrot head-

dress, was conferring with the hat-check girl. His intent was plainly heterosexual; Bech's head reeled at such duplicity. Though they added the weight of his coat to him, he rose like a balloon up the yellow stairs, bumped out through the green door, and stood beneath the street lamp inhaling volumes of the blue Rumanian night.

He felt duty-bound to confront the other writer. They stood, the two of them, on the cobbled pavement, as if on opposite sides of a transparent wall one side of which was lacquered with Scotch and the other with vodka. The other's rimless glasses were misted and the resemblance to Teddy Roosevelt had been dissipated. Bech asked him, "What do you write about?"

The wife, patting her nose with a handkerchief and struggling not to cough, translated the question, and the answer, which was brief. "Peasants," she told Bech. "He wants to know, what do *you* write about?"

Bech spoke to him directly. *"La bourgeoisie,"* he said; and that completed the cultural exchange. Gently bumping and rocking, the writer's car took Bech back to his hotel, where he fell into the deep, unapologetic sleep of the sated.

The plane to Sofia left Bucharest the next morning. Petrescu and the ashen-faced chauffeur came into the tall *fin-de-siècle* dining room for Bech while he was still eating breakfast—*jus d'orange, des croissants*

avec du beurre and *une omelette aux fines herbes.*
Petrescu explained that the driver had gone back to
the theatre, and waited until the ushers and the
managers left, after midnight. But the driver did
not seem resentful, and gave Bech, in the sallow
morning light, a fractional smile, a *risus sardonicus,*
in which his eyes did not participate. On the way
to the airport, he scattered a flock of chickens an
old woman was coaxing across the road, and forced
a military transport truck onto the shoulder, while
its load of soldiers gestured and jeered. Bech's stomach groveled, bathing the fine herbs of his breakfast
in acid. The ceaseless tapping of the horn seemed
a gnawing on all of his nerve ends. Petrescu made
a fastidious mouth and sighed through his nostrils.
"I regret," he said, "that we did not make more occasion to discuss your exciting contemporaries."

"I never read them. They're too exciting," Bech
said, as a line of uniformed schoolchildren was narrowly missed, and a fieldworker with a wheelbarrow
shuffled to safety, spilling potatoes. The day was
overcast above the loamy sunken fields and the roadside trees in their skirts of white paint. "Why," he
asked, not having meant to be rude, "are all these
tree trunks painted?"

"So they are," Petrescu said, "I have not noticed
this before, in all my years. Presumably it is a measure to defeat the insects."

The driver spoke in Rumanian, and Petrescu told
Bech, "He says it is for the car headlights, at night.
Always he is thinking about his job."

At the airport, all the Americans were there who had tried to meet Bech four day ago. Petrescu immediately delivered to Phillips, like a bribe, the name of the writer they had met last night, and Phillips said to Bech, "You spent the evening with *him?* That's fabulous. He's the top of the list, man. We've never laid a finger on him before; he's been inaccessible."

"Stocky guy with glasses?" Bech asked, shielding his eyes. Phillips was so pleased it was like a bright light too early in the day.

"That's the boy. For our money he's the hottest Red writer this side of Solzhenitsyn. He's *waaay* out. Stream of consciousness, no punctuation, everything. There's even some sex."

"You might say he's Red hot," Bech said.

"Huh? Yeah, that's good. Seriously, what did he say to you?"

"He said he'll defect to the West as soon as his shirts come back from the laundry."

"And we went," Petrescu said, "to La Caverne Bleue."

"Say," Phillips said, "you really went underground."

"I think of myself," Bech said modestly, "as a sort of low-flying U-2."

"All kidding aside, Henry"—and here Phillips took Bech by the arms and squeezed—"it sounds as if you've done a sensational job for us. Sensational. Thanks, friend."

Bech hugged everyone in parting—Phillips, the

chargé d'affaires, the junior chargé d'affaires, the ambassador's twelve-year-old nephew, who was taking archery lessons near the airport and had to be dropped off. Bech saved Petrescu for last, and walloped his back, for the man had led him to remember, what he was tempted to forget in America, that reading can be the best part of a man's life.

"I'll send you razor blades," he promised, for in the embrace Petrescu's beard had scratched.

"No, no, I already buy the best. Send me books, any books!"

The plane was roaring to go, and only when safely, or fatally, sealed inside did Bech remember the chauffeur. In the flurry of formalities and baggage handling there had been no goodbye. Worse, there had been no tip. The leu notes Bech had set aside were still folded in his wallet, and his start of guilt gave way, as the runways and dark fields tilted and dwindled under him, to a vengeful satisfaction and glad sense of release. Clouds blotted out the country. He realized that for four days he had been afraid. The man next to him, a portly Slav whose bald brow was beaded with apprehensive sweat, turned and confided something unintelligible, and Bech said, *"Pardon, je ne comprends pas. Je suis Américain."*

The Bulgarian Poetess

Y OUR POEMS. Are they difficult?"

She smiled and, unaccustomed to speaking English, answered carefully, drawing a line in the air with two delicately pinched fingers holding an imaginary pen. "They are difficult—to write."

He laughed, startled and charmed. "But not to read?"

She seemed puzzled by his laugh, but did not withdraw her smile, though its corners deepened in a defensive, feminine way. "I think," she said, "not so very."

"Good." Brainlessly he repeated "Good," disarmed by her unexpected quality of truth. He was, himself, a writer, this fortyish young man, Henry Bech, with his thinning curly hair and melancholy Jewish nose, the author of one good book and three others, the good one having come first. By a kind of oversight, he had never married. His reputation had grown

61

while his powers declined. As he felt himself sink, in his fiction, deeper and deeper into eclectic sexuality and bravura narcissism, as his search for plain truth carried him further and further into treacherous realms of fantasy and, lately, of silence, he was more and more thickly hounded by homage, by flat-footed exegetes, by arrogantly worshipful undergraduates who had hitchhiked a thousand miles to touch his hand, by querulous translators, by election to honorary societies, by invitations to lecture, to "speak," to "read," to participate in symposia trumped up by ambitious girlie magazines in shameless conjunction with venerable universities. His very government, in airily unstamped envelopes from Washington, invited him to travel, as an ambassador of the arts, to the other half of the world, the hostile, mysterious half. Rather automatically, but with some faint hope of shaking himself loose from the burden of himself, he consented, and found himself floating, with a passport so stapled with visas it fluttered when pulled from his pocket, down into the dim airports of Communist cities.

He arrived in Sofia the day after a mixture of Bulgarian and African students had smashed the windows of the American legation and ignited an overturned Chevrolet. The cultural officer, pale from a sleepless night of guard duty, tamping his pipe with trembling fingers, advised Bech to stay out of crowds and escorted him to his hotel. The lobby was swarming with Negroes in black wool fezzes and pointed European shoes. Insecurely disguised, he felt, by an astrakhan hat purchased in Moscow, Bech passed through to the elevator, whose operator addressed him in German. "*Ja, vier,*" Bech answered, "*danke,*" and telephoned, in his bad French, for dinner to be brought up to his room. He remained there all night, behind a locked door, reading Hawthorne. He had lifted a paperback collection of short stories from a legation window sill littered with broken glass. A few curved bright crumbs fell from between the pages onto his blanket. The image of Roger Malvin lying alone, dying, in the forest— "Death would come like the slow approach of a corpse, stealing gradually towards him through the forest, and showing its ghastly and motionless features from behind a nearer and yet a nearer tree"— frightened him. Bech fell asleep early and suffered from swollen, homesick dreams. It had been the first day of Hanukkah.

In the morning, venturing downstairs for breakfast, he was surprised to find the restaurant open, the waiters affable, the eggs actual, the coffee hot, though syrupy. Outside, Sofia was sunny and (except for a few dark glances at his big American shoes) amenable to his passage along the streets. Lozenge-patterns of pansies, looking flat and brittle as pressed flowers, had been set in the public beds. Women with a touch of Western *chic* walked hatless in the park behind the mausoleum of Georgi Dimitrov. There was a mosque, and an assortment of trolley cars salvaged from the remotest corner of Bech's childhood, and a tree that talked—that is, it was so full of birds that it swayed under their weight and emitted volumes of chirping sound like a great leafy loudspeaker. It was the inverse of his hotel, whose silent walls presumably contained listening microphones. Electricity was somewhat enchanted in the Socialist world. Lights flickered off untouched and radios turned themselves on. Telephones rang in the dead of the night and breathed wordlessly in his ear. Six weeks ago, flying from New York City, Bech had expected Moscow to be a blazing counterpart and instead saw, through the plane window, a skein of hoarded lights no brighter, on that vast black plain, than a girl's body in a dark room.

Past the talking tree was the American legation. The sidewalk, heaped with broken glass, was roped off, so that pedestrians had to detour into the gutter. Bech detached himself from the stream, crossed the little barren of pavement, smiled at the Bulgarian militiamen who were sullenly guarding the jewel-bright heaps of shards, and pulled open the bronze door. The cultural officer was crisper after a normal night's sleep. He clenched his pipe in his teeth and handed Bech a small list. "You're to meet with the Writers' Union at eleven. These are writers you might ask to see. As far as we can tell, they're among the more progressive."

Words like "progressive" and "liberal" had a somewhat reversed sense in this world. At times, indeed, Bech felt he had passed through a mirror, a dingy flecked mirror that reflected feebly the capitalist world; in its dim depths everything was similar but left-handed. One of the names ended in "-ova." Bech said, "A woman."

"A poetess," the cultural officer said, sucking and tamping in a fury of bogus efficiency. "Very popular, apparently. Her books are impossible to buy."

"Have you read anything by these people?"

"I'll be frank with you. I can just about make my way through a newspaper."

"But you always know what a newspaper will say anyway."

"I'm sorry, I don't get your meaning."

"There isn't any." Bech didn't quite know why the Americans he met irritated him—whether because they garishly refused to blend into this shadow-world or because they were always so solemnly sending him on ridiculous errands.

At the Writers' Union, he handed the secretary the list as it had been handed to him, on U.S. legation stationery. The secretary, a large stooped man with the hands of a stonemason, grimaced and shook his head but obligingly reached for the telephone. Bech's meeting was already waiting in another room. It was the usual one, the one that, with small differences, he had already attended in Moscow and Kiev, Yerevan and Alma-Ata, Bucharest and Prague: the polished oval table, the bowl of fruit, the morning light, the gleaming glasses of brandy and mineral water, the lurking portrait of Lenin, the six or eight patiently sitting men who would leap to their feet with quick blank smiles. These men would include a few literary officials, termed "critics," high in the Party, loquacious and witty and destined to propose a toast to international understanding; a few selected novelists and poets, mustachioed, smoking, sulking at this invasion of their time; a university professor, the head of the Anglo-American Literature department, speaking in a beautiful withered English of Mark Twain and Sinclair Lewis; a young interpreter with a moist handshake; a shaggy old journalist obsequiously scribbling notes; and, on the rim of the group, in chairs placed to suggest that they had invited themselves, one or two gentlemen of ill-defined status, fidgety and tieless, maverick translators who would turn out to be the only ones present who had ever read a word by Henry Bech.

Here this type was represented by a stout man in a tweed coat leather-patched at the elbows in the British style. The whites of his eyes were distinctly red. He shook Bech's hand eagerly, made of it almost an embrace of reunion, bending his face so close that Bech could distinguish the smells of tobacco, garlic, cheese, and alcohol. Even as they were seating themselves around the table, and the Writers' Union chairman, a man elegantly bald, with very pale eyelashes, was touching his brandy glass as if to lift it, this anxious red-eyed interloper blurted at Bech, "Your *Travel Light* was so marvelous a book. The motels, the highways, the young girls with their lovers who were motorcyclists, so marvelous, so American, the youth, the adoration

66

for space and speed, the barbarity of the advertisements in neon lighting, the very poetry. It takes us truly into another dimension."

Travel Light was the first novel, the famous one. Bech disliked discussing it. "At home," he said, "it was criticized as despairing."

The man's hands, stained orange with tobacco, lifted in amazement and plopped noisily to his knees. "No, no, a thousand times. Truth, wonder, terror even, vulgarity, yes. But despair, no, not at all, not one iota. Your critics are dead wrong."

"Thank you."

The chairman softly cleared his throat and lifted his glass an inch from the table, so that it formed with its reflection a kind of playing card.

Bech's admirer excitedly persisted. "You are not a *wet* writer, no. You are a dry writer, yes? You have the expressions, am I wrong in English, dry, hard?"

"More or less."

"I want to translate you!"

It was the agonized cry of a condemned man, for the chairman coldly lifted his glass to the height of his eyes, and like a firing squad the others followed suit. Blinking his white lashes, the chairman gazed mistily in the direction of the sudden silence, and spoke in Bulgarian.

The young interpreter murmured in Bech's ear. "I wish to propose now, ah, a very brief toast. I know it will seem doubly brief to our honored American guest, who has so recently enjoyed the, ah, hospitality of our Soviet comrades." There must have been a joke here, for the rest of the table laughed. "But in seriousness permit me to say that in our country we have seen in years past too few Americans, ah, of Mr. Bech's progressive and sympathetic stripe. We hope in the next hour to learn from him much that is interesting and, ah, socially useful about the literature of his large country, and perhaps we may in turn inform him of our own proud literature, of which perhaps he knows regrettably little. Ah, so let me finally, then, since there is a saying that too long a courtship spoils the marriage, offer to drink, in our native plum brandy *slivovica*, ah, firstly to the success of his visit and, in the second place, to the mutual increase of international understanding."

"Thank you," Bech said and, as a courtesy, drained his glass. It was wrong; the others, having merely sipped, stared. The purple burning revolved in Bech's stomach and a severe distaste for himself, for his role, for this entire artificial and futile process, focused into a small brown spot on a pear in the bowl so shiningly posed before his eyes.

The red-eyed fool smelling of cheese was ornamenting the toast. "It is a personal honor for me to meet the man who, in *Travel Light*, truly added a new dimension to American prose."

"The book was written," Bech said, "ten years ago."

"And since?" A slumping, mustached man sat up and sprang into English. "Since, you have written what?"

Bech had been asked that question often in these

68

weeks and his answer had grown curt. "A second novel called *Brother Pig*, which is St. Bernard's expression for the body."

"Good. Yes, and?"

"A collection of essays and sketches called *When the Saints*."

"I like the title less well."

"It's the beginning of a famous Negro song."

"We know the song," another man said, a smaller man, with the tense, dented mouth of a hare. He lightly sang, "Lordy, I just want to be in that number."

"And the last book," Bech said, "was a long novel called *The Chosen* that took five years to write and that nobody liked."

"I have read reviews," the red-eyed man said. "I have not read the book. Copies are difficult here."

"I'll give you one," Bech said.

The promise seemed, somehow, to make the recipient unfortunately conspicuous; bringing his stained hands, he appeared to swell in size, to intrude grotesquely upon the inner ring, so that the interpreter took it upon himself to whisper, with the haste of an apology, into Bech's ear, "This gentleman is well known as the translator into our language of *Alice in Wonderland*."

"A marvelous book," the translator said, deflating in relief, pulling at his pockets for a cigarette. "It truly takes us into another dimension. Something that must be done. We live in a new cosmos."

The chairman spoke in Bulgarian, musically, at

length. There was polite laughter. Nobody translated for Bech. The professorial type, his hair like a flaxen toupee, jerked forward. "Tell me, is it true, as I have read"—his phrases whistled slightly, like rusty machinery—"that the stock of Sinclair Lewis has plummeted under the Salinger wave?"

And so it went, here as in Kiev, Prague, and Alma-Ata, the same questions, more or less predictable, and his own answers, terribly familiar to him by now, mechanical, stale, irrelevant, untrue, claustrophobic. Then the door opened. In came, with the rosy air of a woman fresh from a bath, a little breathless, having hurried, hatless, a woman in a blond coat, her hair also blond. The secretary, entering behind her, seemed to make a cherishing space around her with his large curved hands. He introduced her to Bech as Vera Something-ova, the poetess he had asked to meet. None of the others on the list, he explained, had answered their telephones.

"Aren't you kind to come?" As Bech asked it, it was a genuine question, to which he expected some sort of an answer.

She spoke to the interpreter in Bulgarian. "She says," the interpreter told Bech, "she is sorry she is so late."

"But she was just called!" In the warmth of his confusion and pleasure Bech turned to speak directly to her, forgetting he would not be understood. "I'm terribly sorry to have interrupted your morning."

"I am pleased," she said, "to meet you. I heard of you spoken in France."

"You speak English!"

"No. Very little amount."

"But you *do*."

A chair was brought for her from a corner of the room. She yielded her coat, revealing herself in a suit also blond, as if her clothes were an aspect of a total consistency. She sat down opposite Bech, crossing her legs. Her legs were visibly good; her face was perceptibly broad. Lowering her lids, she tugged her skirt to the curve of her knee. It was his sense of her having hurried, hurried to *him*, and of being, still, graciously flustered, that most touched him.

He spoke to her very clearly, across the fruit, fearful of abusing and breaking the fragile bridge of her English. "You are a poetess. When I was young, I also wrote poems."

She was silent so long he thought she would never answer; but then she smiled and pronounced, "You are not old now."

"Your poems. Are they difficult?"

"They are difficult—to write."

"But not to read?"

"I think—not so very."

"Good. Good."

Despite the decay of his career, Bech had retained an absolute faith in his instincts; he never doubted that somewhere an ideal course was open to him and that his intuitions were pre-dealt clues

71

to his destiny. He had loved, briefly or long, with or
without consummation, perhaps a dozen women;
yet all of them, he now saw, shared the trait of ap-
proximation, of narrowly missing an undisclosed
prototype. The surprise he felt did not have to do
with the appearance, at last, of this central woman;
he had always expected her to appear. What he had
not expected was her appearance here, in this remote and abused nation, in this room of morning
light, where he discovered a small knife in his fingers and on the table before him, golden and moist,
a precisely divided pear.

Men traveling alone develop a romantic vertigo.
Bech had already fallen in love with a freckled
embassy wife in Prague, a buck-toothed chanteuse
in Rumania, a stolid Mongolian sculptress in
Kazakhstan. In the Tretyakov Gallery he had fallen
in love with a recumbent statue, and at the Moscow
Ballet School with an entire roomful of girls. Entering the room, he had been struck by the aroma,
tenderly acrid, of young female sweat. Sixteen and
seventeen, wearing patchy practice suits, the girls
were twirling so strenuously their slippers were un-
raveling. Demure student faces crowned the uncon-
scious insolence of their bodies. The room was
doubled in depth by a floor-to-ceiling mirror. Bech
was seated on a bench at its base. Staring above his
head, each girl watched herself with frowning eyes
frozen, for an instant in the turn, by the imperious

delay and snap of her head. Bech tried to remember the lines of Rilke that expressed it, this snap and delay: *did not the drawing remain/that the dark stroke of your eyebrow/swiftly wrote on the wall of its own turning?* At one point the teacher, a shapeless old Ukrainian lady with gold canines, a *prima* of the thirties, had arisen and cried something translated to Bech as, "No, no, the arms free, *free!*" And in demonstration she had executed a rapid series of pirouettes with such proud effortlessness that all the girls, standing this way and that like deer along the wall, had applauded. Bech had loved them for that. In all his loves, there was an urge to rescue—to rescue the girls from the slavery of their exertions, the statue from the cold grip of its own marble, the embassy wife from her boring and unctuous husband, the chanteuse from her nightly humiliation (she could not sing), the Mongolian from her stolid race. But the Bulgarian poetess presented herself to him as needing nothing, as being complete, poised, satisfied, achieved. He was aroused and curious and, the next day, inquired about her of the man with the vaguely contemptuous mouth of a hare—a novelist turned playwright and scenarist, who accompanied him to the Rila Monastery. "She lives to write," the playwright said. "I do not think it is healthy."

Bech said, "But she seems so healthy." They stood beside a small church with whitewashed walls. From the outside it looked like a hovel, a shelter for pigs or chickens. For five centuries the Turks had ruled Bulgaria, and the Christian churches, however richly adorned within, had humble exteriors. A peasant woman with wildly snarled hair unlocked the door for them. Though the church could hardly ever have held more than thirty worshippers, it was divided into three parts, and every inch of wall was covered with eighteenth-century frescoes. Those in the narthex depicted a Hell where the devils wielded scimitars. Passing through the tiny nave, Bech peeked through the iconostasis into the screened area that, in the symbolism of Orthodox architecture, represented the next, the hidden world —Paradise. He glimpsed a row of books, an easy chair, a pair of ancient oval spectacles. Outdoors again, he felt released from the unpleasantly tight atmosphere of a children's book. They were on the side of a hill. Above them was a stand of pines whose trunks were shelled with ice. Below them sprawled the monastery, a citadel of Bulgarian national feeling during the years of the Turkish Yoke. The last monks had been moved out in 1961. An aimless soft rain was falling in these mountains, and there were not many German tourists today. Across the valley, whose little silver river still turned a water wheel, a motionless white horse stood silhouetted against a green meadow, pinned there like a brooch.

"I am an old friend of hers," the playwright said. "I worry about her."

"Are the poems good?"

"It is difficult for me to judge. They are very feminine. Perhaps shallow."

"Shallowness can be a kind of honesty."

74

"Yes. She is very honest in her work."

"And in her life?"

"As well."

"What does her husband do?"

The other man looked at him with parted lips and touched his arm, a strange Slavic gesture, communicating an underlying racial urgency, that Bech no longer shied from. "But she has no husband. As I say, she is too much for poetry to have married."

"But her name ends in '-ova.'"

"I see. You are mistaken. It is not a matter of marriage; I am Petrov, my unmarried sister is Petrova. All females."

"How stupid of me. But I think it's such a pity, she's so charming."

"In America, only the uncharming fail to marry?"

"Yes, you must be very uncharming not to marry."

"It is not so here. The government indeed is alarmed; our birth rate is one of the lowest in Europe. It is a problem for economists."

Bech gestured at the monastery. "Too many monks?"

"Not enough, perhaps. With too few of monks, something of the monk enters everybody."

The peasant woman, who seemed old to Bech but who was probably younger than he, saw them to the edge of her domain. She huskily chattered in what Petrov said was very amusing rural slang. Behind her, now hiding in her skirts and now darting away, was her child, a boy not more than three. He was faithfully chased, back and forth, by a small white pig, who moved, as pigs do, on tiptoe, with remarkably abrupt changes of direction. Something in the scene, in the open glee of the woman's parting smile and the unself-conscious way her hair thrust out from her head, something in the mountain mist and spongy rutted turf into which frost had begun to break at night, evoked for Bech a nameless absence to which was attached, like a horse to a meadow, the image of the poetess, with her broad face, her good legs, her Parisian clothes, and her sleekly brushed hair. Petrov, in whom he was beginning to sense, through the wraps of foreignness, a clever and kindred mind, seemed to have overheard his thoughts, for he said, "If you would like, we could have dinner. It would be easy for me to arrange."

"With her?"

"Yes, she is my friend, she would be glad."

"But I have nothing to say to her. I'm just curious about such an intense conjunction of good looks and brains. I mean, what does a soul do with it all?"

"You may ask her. Tomorrow night?"

"I'm sorry, I can't. I'm scheduled to go to the ballet, and the next night the legation is giving a cocktail party for me, and then I fly home."

"Home? So soon?"

"It does not feel soon to me. I must try to work again."

"A drink, then. Tomorrow evening before the ballet? It is possible? It is not possible."

Petrov looked puzzled, and Bech realized that it

was his fault, for he was nodding to say Yes, but in Bulgarian nodding meant No, and a shake of the head meant Yes. "Yes," he said. "Gladly."

The ballet was entitled *Silver Slippers*. As Bech watched it, the word "ethnic" kept coming to his mind. He had grown accustomed, during his trip, to this sort of artistic evasion, the retreat from the difficult and disappointing present into folk dance, folk tale, folk song, with always the implication that, beneath the embroidered peasant costume, the folk was really one's heart's own darling, the proletariat.

"Do you like fairy tales?" It was the moist-palmed interpreter who accompanied him to the theatre.

"I *love* them," Bech said, with a fervor and gaiety lingering from the previous hour. The interpreter looked at him anxiously, as when Bech had swallowed the brandy in one swig, and throughout the ballet kept murmuring explanations of self-evident events on the stage. Each night, a princess would put on silver slippers and dance through her mirror to tryst with a wizard, who possessed a magic stick that she coveted, for with it the world could be ruled. The wizard, as a dancer, was inept, and once almost dropped her, so that anger flashed from her eyes. She was, the princess, a little redhead with a high round bottom and a frozen pout and beautiful free arm motions, and Bech found it oddly ecstatic when, preparatory to her leap, she would dance toward the mirror, an empty oval, and another girl, identically dressed in pink, would emerge from the wings and perform as her reflection. And when the princess, haughtily adjusting her cape of invisibility, leaped through the oval of gold wire, Bech's heart leaped backward into the enchanted hour he had spent with the poetess.

Though the appointment had been established, she came into the restaurant as if, again, she had been suddenly summoned and had hurried. She sat down between Bech and Petrov slightly breathless and fussed, but exuding, again, that impalpable warmth of intelligence and virtue.

"Vera, Vera," Petrov said.

"You hurry too much," Bech told her.

"Not so very much," she said.

Petrov ordered her a cognac and continued with Bech their discussion of the newer French novelists. "It is tricks," Petrov said. "Good tricks, but tricks. It does not have enough to do with life, it is too much verbal nervousness. Is that sense?"

"It's an epigram," Bech said.

"There are just two of their number with whom I do not feel this: Claude Simon and Samuel Beckett. You have no relation, Bech, Beckett?"

"None."

Vera said, "Nathalie Sarraute is a very modest woman. She felt motherly to me."

"You have met her?"

"In Paris I heard her speak. Afterward there was the coffee. I liked her theories, of the, oh, *what*? Of the *little* movements within the heart." She delicately measured a pinch of space and smiled, through Bech, back at herself.

"Tricks," Petrov said. "I do not feel this with Beckett; there, in a low form, believe it or not, one has human content."

Bech felt duty-bound to pursue this, to ask about the theatre of the absurd in Bulgaria, about abstract painting (these were the touchstones of "progressiveness"; Russia had none, Rumania some, Czechoslovakia plenty), to subvert Petrov. Instead, he asked the poetess, "Motherly?"

Vera explained, her hands delicately modeling the air, rounding into nuance, as it were, the square corners of her words. "After her talk, we—talked."

"In French?"

"And in Russian."

"She knows Russian?"

"She was born Russian."

"How is her Russian?"

"Very pure but—old-fashioned. Like a book. As she talked, I felt in a book, safe."

"You do not always feel safe?"

"Not always."

"Do you find it difficult to be a woman poet?"

"We have a tradition of woman poets. We have Elisaveta Bagriana, who is very great."

Petrov leaned toward Bech as if to nibble him. "Your own works? Are they influenced by the *nouvelle vague*? Do you consider yourself to write anti-*romans*?"

Bech kept himself turned toward the woman. "Do

you want to hear about how I write? You don't, do you?"

"Very much yes," she said.

He told them, told them shamelessly, in a voice that surprised him with its steadiness, its limpid urgency, how once he had written, how in *Travel Light* he had sought to show people skimming the surface of things with their lives, taking tints from things the way that objects in a still life color one another, and how later he had attempted to place beneath the melody of plot a countermelody of imagery, interlocking images which had risen to the top and drowned his story, and how in *The Chosen* he had sought to make of this confusion the theme itself, an epic theme, by showing a population of characters whose actions were all determined, at the deepest level, by nostalgia, by a desire to get back, to dive, each, into the springs of their private imagery. The book probably failed; at least, it was badly received. Bech apologized for telling all this. His voice tasted flat in his mouth; he felt a secret intoxication and a secret guilt, for he had contrived to give a grand air, as of an impossibly noble and quixotically complex experiment, to his failure when at bottom, he suspected, a certain simple laziness was the cause.

Petrov said, "Fiction so formally sentimental could not be composed in Bulgaria. We do not have a happy history."

It was the first time Petrov had sounded like a Communist. If there was one thing that irked Bech about these people behind the mirror, it was their assumption that, however second-rate elsewhere, in suffering they were supreme. He said, "Believe it or not, neither do we."

Vera calmly intruded. "Your personae are not moved by love?"

"Yes, very much. But as a form of nostalgia. We fall in love, I tried to say in the book, with women who remind us of our first landscape. A silly idea. I used to be interested in love. I once wrote an essay on the orgasm—you know the word?—"

She shook her head. He remembered that it meant Yes.

"—on the orgasm as perfect memory. The one mystery is, what are we remembering?"

She shook her head again, and he noticed that her eyes were gray, and that in their depths his image (which he could not see) was searching for the thing remembered. She composed her finger tips around the brandy glass and said, "There is a French poet, a young one, who has written of this. He says that never else do we, do we so gather up, collect into ourselves, oh—" Vexed, she spoke to Petrov in rapid Bulgarian.

He shrugged and said, "Concentrate our attention."

"—concentrate our attention," she repeated to Bech, as if the words, to be believed, had to come from her. "I say it foolish—foolishly—but in French it is very well put and—*correct*."

Petrov smiled neatly and said, "This is an enjoyable subject for discussion, love."

"It remains," Bech said, picking his words as if the language were not native even to him, "one of the few things that still deserve meditation."

"I think it is good," she said.

"Love?" he asked, startled.

She shook her head and tapped the stem of her glass with a fingernail, so that Bech had an inaudible sense of ringing, and she bent as if to study the liquor, so that her entire body borrowed a rosiness from the brandy and burned itself into Bech's memory—the silver gloss of her nail, the sheen of her hair, the symmetry of her arms relaxed on the white tablecloth, everything except the expression on her face. Petrov asked aloud Bech's opinion of Dürrenmatt.

Actuality is a running impoverishment of possibility. Though he had looked forward to seeing her again at the cocktail party and had made sure that she was invited, when it occurred, though she came, he could not get to her. He saw her enter, with Petrov, but he was fenced in by an attaché of the Yugoslav Embassy and his burnished Tunisian wife; and, later, when he was worming his way toward her diagonally, a steely hand closed on his arm and a rasping American female told him that her fifteen-year-old nephew had decided to be a writer and desperately needed advice. Not the standard crap, but real brass-knuckles advice. Bech found himself balked. He was surrounded by America: the voices, the narrow suits, the watery drinks, the clatter, the glitter. The mirror had gone opaque and gave him back only himself. He managed, in the end, as the officials were thinning out, to break through and confront her in a corner. Her coat, blond, with a rabbit collar, was already on; from its side pocket she pulled a pale volume of poems in the Cyrillic alphabet. "Please," she said. On the flyleaf she had written, "to H. Beck, sincerelly, with bad spellings but much"—the last word looked like "leave" but must have been "love."

"Wait," he begged, and went back to where his ravaged pile of presentation books had been and, unable to find the one he wanted, stole the legation library's jacketless copy of *The Chosen*. Placing it in her expectant hands, he told her, "Don't look," for inside he had written, with a drunk's stylistic confidence,

Dear Vera Glavanakova—
It is a matter of earnest regret for me that you and I must live on opposite sides of the world.

Bech Takes Pot Luck

Though Henry Bech's few persistent admirers among the critics praised his "highly individual and refractory romanticism," his "stubborn refusal to mount, in this era of artistic coup d'état and herd movement, any bandwagon but that of his own quixotic, excessively tender, strangely anti-Semitic Semitic sensibility," the author nevertheless had a sneaking fondness for the fashionable. Each August, he deserted his shabby large apartment at Ninety-ninth and Riverside and rented a cottage on a Massachusetts island whose coves and sandy lanes were crammed with other writers, television producers, museum directors, under-secretaries of State, old *New Masses* editors possessively squatting on seaside acreage bought for a song in the Depression, movie stars whose forties films were now enjoying a Camp revival, and hordes of those handsome, entertaining, professionless prosperous who fill the chinks between celebrities. It innocently delighted Bech, a child of the lower middle class, to see these luxurious people padding in bare feet along the dirty sidewalks of the island's one town, or fighting for overpriced groceries in the tiny general store of an up-island hamlet. It gratified him to recognize some literary idol of his youth, shrunken and frail, being tumbled about by the surf; or to be himself recognized by some faunlike bikinied girl who had been assigned *Travel Light* at the Brearley School, or by a cozy Westchester matron, still plausible in her scoop-back one-piece, who amiably confused Bech's controversial chef-d'œuvre *The Chosen* with a contemporary best-seller of the same title. Though often thus accosted, Bech had never before been intercepted by a car. The little scarlet Porsche, the long blond hair of its driver flapping, cut in front of Bech's old Ford as he was driving to the beach, and forced him to brake within inches of two mailboxes painted with flowers and lettered, respectively, "Sea Shanty" and "Avec du Sel." The boy—it was a boy's long blond hair—hopped out and raced back to Bech's window, extending a soft hand that, as Bech docilely shook it, trembled like a bird's breast. The boy's plump face seemed falsified by the uncut mane; it engulfed his ears and gave his mouth, perhaps because it was unmistakably male, an assertive quarrelsome look. His eyebrows were sunbleached to invisibility; his pallid blue eyes were all wonder and love.

"Mr. Bech, hey. I couldn't believe it was you."

"Suppose it hadn't been me. How would you explain forcing me into this ditch?"

"I bet you don't remember who I am."

"Let me guess. You're not Sabu, and you're not Freddie Bartholomew."

"Wendell Morrison, Mr. Bech. English 1020 at Columbia, 1963." For one spring term Bech, who belonged to the last writing generation that thought teaching a corruption, had been persuaded to oversee—it amounted to little more than that—the remarkably uninhibited conversations of fifteen undergraduates and to read their distressingly untidy manuscripts. Languid and clever, these young people had lacked not only patriotism and faith but even the coarse morality competitiveness imposes. Living off fathers they despised, systematically attracted to the outrageous, they seemed ripe for Fascism. Their politics burlesqued the liberal beliefs dear to Bech; their literary tastes ran to chaotic second-raters like Miller and Tolkien and away from those saints of formalism—Eliot, Valéry, Joyce—whose humble suppliant Bech had been. Bech even found fault with them physically: though the girls were taller and better endowed than the girls of his youth, with neater teeth and clearer skins, there was something doughy about their beauty; the starved, conflicted girls of Bech's generation had had distinctly better legs. He slowly remembered Wendell. The boy always sat on Bech's left, a fair-haired young Wasp from Stamford, crewcut, a Connecticut Yankee, more grave and respectful than the others, indeed so courteous Bech wondered if some kind of irony were intended. He appeared to adore Bech; and Bech's weakness for Wasps was well known. "You wrote in lower case," Bech said. "An orgy with some girls in a house full of expensive furniture. Glints of pink flesh in a chandelier. Somebody defecated on a polar-bear rug."

"That's right. What a great memory."

"Only for fantasies."

"You gave it an A, you said it really shook you up. That meant a hell of a lot to me. I couldn't tell you then, I was playing it cool, that was my hang-up, but I can tell you now, Mr. Bech, it was real encouragement, it's really kept me going. You were great."

As the loosening of the boy's vocabulary indicated a prolonged conversation, the woman beside Bech shifted restlessly. Wendell's clear blue eyes observed the movement, and obligated Bech to perform introductions. "Norma, this is Wendell Morris. Miss Norma Latchett."

"Morrison," the boy said, and reached in past Bech's nose to shake Norma's hand. "He's beautiful, isn't he, Ma'am?"

She answered dryly, "He'll do." Her thin brown hand rested in Wendell's white plump one as if stranded. It was a sticky day.

"Let's *go*," a child exclaimed from the back seat, in that dreadful squeezed voice that precedes a tantrum. Helplessly Bech's hands tightened on the steering wheel, and the hairs on the back of his neck stiffened. After two weeks, he was still unacclimated

to the pressures of surrogate paternity. The child
grunted, stuffed with fury; Bech's stomach sympa-
thetically clenched.

"Hush," the child's mother said, slow-voiced,
soothing. "Uncle Harry's talking to an old student of
his. They haven't seen each other for years."

Wendell bent low to peer into the back seat, and
Bech was obliged to continue introductions. "This is
Norma's sister, Mrs. Beatrice Cook, and her children
—Ann, Judy, Donald."

Wendell nodded four times in greeting. His furry
plump hand clung tenaciously to the sill of Bech's
window. "Quite a scene," he said.

Bech told him, "We're trying to get to the beach
before it clouds over." Every instant, the sky grew
less transparent. Often the island was foggy while
the mainland, according to the radio, blissfully
baked.

"Where's everybody staying?" The boy's assumption that they were all living together irritated Bech,
since it was correct.

"We've rented a shoe," Bech said, "from an old
lady who's moved up to a cigar box."

Wendell's eyes lingered on the three fair children
crammed, along with sand pails and an inflated air
mattress, into the back seat beside their mother. He
asked them, "Uncle Harry's quite a card, huh, kids?"

Bech imagined he had hurt Wendell's feelings. In
rapid atonement he explained, "We're in a cottage
rented from Andy Spofford, who used to be in war
movies—before your time, he played sidekicks that

got killed—and lives mostly in Corsica now. Blue mailbox, third dirt road past the Up-Island Boutique, take every left turning except the last, when you go right, not *hard* right. Mrs. Cook is up from Ossining visiting for the week." Bech restrained himself from telling Wendell that she was going through a divorce and cried every evening and lived on pills. Bea was an unspectacular middle-sized woman two years younger than Norma; she wore dull clothes that seemed designed to set off her sister's edgy beauty.

Wendell understood Bech's apologetic burst as an invitation, and removed his hand from the door. "Hey, I know this is an imposition, but I'd love to have you just glance at the stuff I'm doing now. I'm out of that lower-case bag. In fact I'm into something pretty classical. I've seen the movie of *Ulysses* twice."

"And you've let your hair grow. You're out of the barbershop bag."

Wendell spoke past Bech's ear to the children. "You kids like to Sunfish?"

"Yes!" Ann and Judy chorused; they were twins.

"What's Sunfish?" Donald asked.

Going to the beach had been the children's only entertainment. Their mother was drugged and dazed, Norma detested physical activity before dark, and Bech was frightened of the water. Even the ferry ride over to the island felt precarious to him. He never sailed, and rarely swam in water higher than his hips. From his apartment on Riverside Drive, he looked across to New Jersey as if the Hudson were a wide flat black street.

"Let's do it tomorrow," Wendell said. "I'll come for them around one, if that's O.K., Ma'am."

Bea, flustered to find herself addressed—for Bech and Norma had almost enforced invisibility upon her, staging their fights and reconciliations as if she were not in the cottage—answered in her melodious grief-slowed voice, "That would be lovely of you, if you really want to bother. Is there any danger?"

"Not a bit, ma'am. I have life jackets. I used to be a camp councilor."

"That must have been when you shot your polar bear," Bech said, and pointedly restarted the motor.

They arrived at the beach just as the sun went behind one of those irregular expanding clouds whose edges hold blue sky at bay for hours. The children, jubilant at freedom and the prospect of Sunfishing, plunged into the surf. Norma, as if unwrapping a fragile gift in faintly poor taste, removed her beach robe, revealing a mauve bikini, and, inserting plastic eyecups in her sockets, arranged herself in the center of a purple towel the size of a double bed. Bea, disconsolate in a loose brown suit that did not do her figure justice, sat down on the sand with a book— one of Bech's, curiously. Though her sister had been his mistress for two and a half years, she had just got around to doing her homework. Embarrassed, fearful that the book, so near his actual presence, would somehow detonate, Bech moved off a few strides and stood, bare-chested, gazing at his splendid enemy the sea, an oblivious hemisphere whose glitter of whitecaps sullenly persisted without the sun. Shortly, a timid adolescent voice, the voice he had been waiting for, rustled at his shoulder. "I beg your pardon, sir, but by any chance are you . . . ?"

Wendell found Bech's diffident directions no obstacle and came for the children promptly at one the next day. The expedition was so successful Beatrice prolonged her visit another week. Wendell took the children clamming and miniature-golfing; he took them to an Indian burial ground, to an abandoned windmill, to grand beaches fenced with No Trespassing signs. The boy had that Wasp knowingness, that facility with things: he knew how to insert a clam knife, how to snorkle (just to put on the mask made Bech gasp for breath), how to bluff and charm his way onto private beaches (Bech believed everything he read), how to excite children with a few broken shell bits that remotely might be remnants of ceremonially heaped conch shells. He was connected to the land in a way Bech could only envy. Though so young, he had been everywhere—Italy, Scandinavia, Mexico, Alaska—whereas Bech, except for Caribbean holidays and a State Department-sponsored excursion to some Communist countries, had hardly been anywhere. He lived twenty blocks north of where he had been born, and couldn't sleep for nervousness the night before he and Norma and his rickety Ford risked the journey up the seaboard to the ferry slip. The continent-spanning motorcyclists of *Travel Light* had been daydreams based upon his Cincinnati sister's complaints about her older son, a college dropout. Wendell, a mere twenty-three, shamed Bech with his Yankee ingenuity, his native woodcraft—the dozen and one tricks of a beach picnic, for instance; the oven of scooped sand, the corn salted in seawater, the fire of scavenged driftwood. It all seemed adventurous to Bech, as did the boy's removal, in the amber summer twilight, of his bathing suit to body-surf. Wendell was a pudgy yet complete Adonis stiff-armed in the waves, his buttocks pearly, his genitals distinctly visible when he stood in the wave troughs. The new generation was immersed in the world that Bech's, like a foolish old bridegroom full of whiskey and dogma, had tried to mount and master. Bech was shy of things, and possessed few, not even a wife; Wendell's room, above a garage on the summer property of some friends of his parents, held everything from canned anchovies and a Bible to pornographic photographs and a gram of LSD.

Ever since Bech had met her, Norma had wanted to take LSD. It was one of her complaints against him that he had never got her any. He, who knew that all her complaints were in truth that he would not marry her, told her she was too old. She was thirty-six; he was forty-three, and, though flirting with the senility that comes early to American authors, still absurdly wary of anything that might damage his brain. When, on their cottage porch, Wendell let slip the fact that he possessed some

LSD, Bech recognized Norma's sudden new mood. Her nose sharpened, her wide mouth rapidly fluctuated between a heart-melting grin and a severe down-drawn look almost of anger. It was the mood in which, two Christmases ago, she had come up to him at a party, ostensibly to argue about *The Chosen,* in fact to conjure him into taking her to dinner. She began to converse exclusively with Wendell.

"Where did you get it?" she asked. "Why haven't you used it?"

"Oh," he said, "I knew a turned-on chemistry major. I've had it for a year now. You just don't take it, you know, before bedtime like Ovaltine. There has to be somebody to take the trip with. It can be very bad business"—he had his solemn whispering voice, behind his boyish naïve one—"to go on a trip alone."

"You've been," Bech said politely.

"I've been." His shadowy tone matched the moment of day. The westward sky was plunging toward rose; the sailboats were taking the final tack toward harbor. Inside the cottage, the children, happy and loud after an expedition with Wendell to the lobster hatchery, were eating supper. Beatrice went in to give them dessert, and to get herself a sweater.

Norma's fine lean legs twitched, recrossing, as she turned to Wendell with her rapacious grin. Before she could speak, Bech asked a question that would restore to himself the center of attention. "And is this what you write about now? In the classic manner of *Ulysses* movies?"

Under the embarrassment of having to instruct his

instructor, Wendell's voice dropped another notch. "It's not really writable. Writing makes distinctions, and this breaks them down. For example, I remember once looking out my window at Columbia. Someone had left a green towel on the gravel roof. From sunbathing, I suppose. I thought, Mmm, pretty green towel, nice shade of green, *beau*tiful shade of green—and the color at*tacked* me!"

Norma asked, "How attacked you? It grew teeth? Grew bigger? What?" She was having difficulty, Bech felt, keeping herself out of Wendell's lap. The boy's innocent eyes, browless as a Teddy bear's, flicked a question toward Bech.

"Tell her," Bech told him. "She's curious."

"I'm *hor*ribly curious," Norma exclaimed. "I'm *so* tired of being myself. Liquor doesn't do anything for me anymore, sex, *any*thing."

Wendell glanced again toward Bech, worried. "It —attacked me. It tried to become me."

"Was it wonderful? Or terrible?"

"It was borderline. You must understand, Norma, it's not a playful experience. It takes everything you have." His tone of voice had become the unnaturally, perhaps ironically, respectful one he had used in English 1020.

"It'll even take," Bech told her, "your Saks charge-a-plate."

Bea appeared in the doorway, dim behind the screen. "As long as I'm on my feet, does anybody want another drink?"

"Oh, *Bea*," Norma said, leaping up, "stop being a martyr. It's my turn to cook, let me help you." To

Bech, before going in, she said, "*Please* arrange my trip with Wendell. He thinks I'm a nuisance, but he *adores* you. Tell him how good I'll be."

Her departure left the men silent. Sheets of mackerel shards were sliding down the sky toward a magenta sunset; Bech felt himself being sucked into a situation where nothing, neither tact nor reason nor the morality he had learned from his father and Flaubert, afforded leverage. Wendell at last asked, "How stable is she?"

"Very un-."

"Any history of psychological disturbance?"

"Nothing but the usual psychiatry. Quit analysis after four months. Does her work apparently quite well—layout and design for an advertising agency. Likes to show her temper off but underneath has a good hard eye on the main chance."

"I'd really need to spend some time alone with her. It's very important that people on a trip together be congenial. They last at least twelve hours. Without rapport, it's a nightmare." The boy was so solemn, so blind to the outrageousness of what he was proposing, that Bech laughed. As if rebuking Bech with his greater seriousness, Wendell whispered in the dusk, "The people you've taken a trip with become the most important people in your life."

"Well," Bech said, "I want to wish you and Norma all the luck in the world. When should we send out announcements?"

Wendell intoned, "I feel you disapprove. I feel your fright."

Bech was speechless. Didn't he know what a mistress was? No sense of private property in this generation. The early Christians; Brook Farm.

Wendell went on carefully, considerately, "Let me propose this. Has she ever smoked pot?"

"Not with me around. I'm an old-fashioned father figure. Two parts Abraham to one part Fagin."

"Why don't she and I, Mr. Bech, smoke some marijuana together as a dry run? That way she can satisfy her female curiosity and I can see if we could stand a trip together. As I size her up, she's much too practical-minded to be a head; she just wants to make the sixties scene, and maybe to bug you."

The boy was so hopeful, so reasonable, that Bech could not help treating him as a student, with all of a student's purchased prerogatives, a student's ruthless power to intrude and demand. Young American minds. The space race with Russia. Bech heard himself yield. "O.K. But you're not taking her over into that sorcerer's-apprentice cubbyhole of yours."

Wendell puzzled; he seemed in the half light a blameless furry creature delicately nosing his way through the inscrutable maze of the other man's prejudices. At last he said, "I think I see your worry. You're wrong. There is absolutely no chance of sex. All these things of course are sexual depressants. It's a medical fact."

Bech laughed again. "Don't you dare sexually depress Norma. It's all she and I have any more." But in making this combination of joke and confession, he had absolved the boy of the maze and admitted him more deeply into his life than he had intended—

all because, Bech suspected, at bottom he was afraid of being out-of-date. They agreed that Wendell would bring back some marijuana and they would give him supper. "You'll have to take pot luck," Bech told him.

Norma was not pleased by his arrangements. "How ridiculous of you," she said, "not to trust me alone with that child. You're so immature and proprietorial. You don't own me. I'm a free agent, by your preference."

"I wanted to save you embarrassment," he told her. "I've read the kid's stories; you don't know what goes on in his mind."

"No, after keeping you company for three years I've forgotten what goes on in any normal man's mind."

"Then you admit he *is* a normal man. *Not* a child. O.K. You stay out of that bastard's atelier, or whatever he thinks it is. A pad."

"My, aren't *you* the fierce young lover? I wonder how I survived thirty-odd years out from under your wing."

"You're so self-destructive, I wonder too. And by the way it's not been three years we've been keeping company, it's two and a half."

"You've been counting the minutes. Is my time about up?"

"Norma, *why* do you want to cop out with all these drugs? It's so insulting to the world, to me."

97

"I want to have an *experience*. I've never had a *baby*, the only wedding ring I've ever worn is the one you loan me when we go to St. Croix in the winter, I've never been to Pakistan, I'm *never* going to get to Antarctica."

"I'll buy you a freezer."

"That *is* your solution, isn't it?—buy another box. You go from box to box, each one snugger than the last. Well I for one *don't* think your marvelous life-style, your heady mixture of art for art's sake and Depression funk, entirely covers the case. My life is closing in and I hate it and I thought this way I could open it up a little. Just a *little*. Just a teeny *crack*, a splinter of sunshine."

"He's coming back, he's coming back. Your fix is on the way."

"How can I *possibly* get high with you and Bea sitting there watching with long faces? It's too grotesque. It's too limiting. My kid sister. My kindly protector. I might as well call my mother—she can fly up from West Orange with the smelling salts."

Bech was grateful to her, for letting her anger, her anguish, recede from the high point reached with the wail that she had never had a baby. He promised, "We'll take it with you."

"Who will? You and Bea?" Norma laughed scornfully. "You two nannies. You're the two most careful people I've ever met."

"We'd *love* to smoke pot. Wouldn't we, Bea? Come on, take a holiday. Break yourself of Nembutal."

Beatrice, who had been cooking lamb chops and

98

setting the table for four while Bech and her sister were obstructively gesturing in the passageway between the kitchen and the dining area, stopped and considered. "Rodney would have a fit."

"Rodney's divorcing you," Bech told her. "Think for yourself."

"It makes it *too* ridiculous," Norma protested. "It takes *all* the adventure out of it."

Bech asked sharply, "Don't you love us?"

"Well," Bea was saying. "On one condition. The children must be asleep. I don't want them to see me do anything wild."

It was Wendell's ingenious idea to have the children sleep on the porch, away from what noise and fumes there might be. He had brought from his magical cache of supplies two sleeping bags, one a double, for the twins. He settled the three small Cooks by pointing out the constellations and the area of the sky where they might, according to this week's newspapers, see shooting stars. "And when you grow tired of that," Wendell said, "close your eyes and listen for an owl."

"Are there owls?" one twin asked.

"Oh, sure."

"On this island?" asked the other.

"One or two. Every island has to have an owl, otherwise the mice would multiply and multiply and there would be no grass, just mice."

"Will it get us?" Donald was the youngest, five.

"You're no mouse," Wendell whispered. "You're a man."

Bech, eavesdropping, felt a pang, and envied the

new Americans their easy intermingling with children. How terrible it seemed for him, a Jew, not to
have children, to lack a father's dignity. The four
adults ate a sober and unconversational meal. Wendell asked Bech what he was writing now, and Bech
said nothing, he was proofreading his old books, and
finding lots of typos. No wonder the critics had mis-
understood him. Norma had changed into a shimmering housecoat, a peacock-colored silk kimono
Bech had bought her last Christmas—their second an-
niversary. He wondered if she had kept on her un-
derclothes, and finally glimpsed, as she bent frowning over her overcooked lamb chop, the reassuring
pale edge of a bra. During coffee, he cleared his
throat. "Well, kids. Should the séance begin?"

Wendell arranged four chairs in a rectangle, and
produced a pipe. It was an ordinary pipe, the kind
that authors, in the corny days when Bech's image
of the literary life had been formed, used to grip on
dust-jacket photographs. Norma took the best chair,
the wicker armchair, and impatiently smoked a
cigarette while Beatrice cleared away the dishes and
checked on the children. They were asleep beneath
the stars. Donald had moved his sleeping bag against
the girls' and lay with his thumb in his mouth and
the other hand on Judy's hair. Beatrice and Bech sat
down, and Wendell spoke to them as if they were
children, showing them the magic substance, which
looked like a residue of pencil shavings in a dirty
tobacco pouch, instructing them how to suck in air
and smoke simultaneously, how to "swallow" the

smoke and hold it down, so the precious narcotic permeated the lungs and stomach and veins and brain. The thoroughness of these instructions aroused in Bech the conviction that something was going to go wrong. He found Wendell as an instructor pompous. In a fury of puffing and expressive inhaling, the boy got the pipe going, and offered first drag to Norma. She had never smoked a pipe, and suffered a convulsion of coughing. Wendell leaned forward and greedily inhaled from midair the smoke she had wasted. He had become, seen sidewise, with his floppy blond hair, a baby lion above a bone; his hungry quick movements were padded with a sinister silence. "Hurry," he hoarsely urged Norma, "don't waste it. It's all I have left from my last trip to Mexico. We may not have enough for four."

She tried again—Bech felt her as tense, rebellious, all too aware that, with the pipe between her teeth, she became a sharp-nosed crone—and coughed again, and complained, "I'm not *getting* any."

Wendell whirled, barefoot, and, stabbing with the pipestem, said, "Mr. Bech."

The smoke was sweet and circular and soft, softer than Bech could have imagined, ballooning in his mouth and throat and chest like a benevolent thunderhead, like one of those valentines from his childhood that unfolded into a three-dimensional tissue-paper fan. "More," Wendell commanded, thrusting the pipe at him again, ravenously sniffing into himself the shreds of smoke that escaped Bech's sucking. This time there was a faint burning—a ghost of tobacco's unkind rasp. Bech felt himself as a domed chamber, with vaults and upward recesses, welcoming the cloud; he shut his eyes. The color of the sensation was yellow mixed with blue yet in no way green. The base of his throat satisfyingly burned.

While his attention was turned inward, Beatrice was given the pipe. Smoke leaked from her compressed lips; it seemed intensely poignant to Bech that even in depravity she was wearing no lipstick. "Give it to *me*," Norma insisted, greedily reaching. Wendell snatched the pipe against his chest and, with the ardor of a trapped man breathing through a tube, inhaled marijuana. The air began to smell sweetish, flowery, and gentle. Norma jumped from her chair and, kimono shimmering, roughly seized the pipe, so that precious sparks flew. Wendell pushed her back into her chair and, like a mother feeding a baby, insinuated the pipestem between her lips. "Gently, gently," he crooned, "take it in, feel it press against the roof of your mouth, blossoming inside you, hold it fast, fast." His s's were extremely sibilant.

"What's all this hypnosis?" Bech asked. He disliked the deft way Wendell handled Norma. The boy swooped to him and eased the wet pipe into his mouth. "Deeper, deeper, that's it, good . . . good . . ."

"It burns," Bech protested.

"It's supposed to," Wendell said. "That's beautiful. You're really getting it."

"Suppose I get sick."

"People never get sick on it, it's a medical fact."

Bech turned to Beatrice and said, "We've raised a generation of amateur pharmacologists."

She had the pipe; handing it back to Wendell, she smiled and pronounced, "Yummy."

Norma kicked her legs and said savagely, "Nothing's *hap*pening. It's not *do*ing anything to me."

"It will, it will," Wendell insisted. He sat down in the fourth chair and passed the pipe. Fine sweat beaded his plump round face.

"Did you ever notice," Bech asked him, "what nifty legs Norma has? She's old enough to be your biological mother, but condescend to take a gander at her gams. We were the Sinewy Generation."

"What's this generation bag you're in?" Wendell asked him, still rather respectfully English 1020. "Everybody's people."

"*Our* biological mother," Beatrice unexpectedly announced, "thought actually *I* had the better figure. She used to call Norma nobby."

"I *won't* sit here being discussed like a piece of meat," Norma said. Grudgingly she passed the pipe to Bech.

As Bech smoked, Wendell crooned, "Yes, deeper, let it fill you. He really has it. My master, my guru."

"Guru you," Bech said, passing the pipe to Beatrice. He spoke with a rolling slowness, sonorous as an idol's voice. "All you flower types are incipient Fascists." The a's and s's had taken on a private richness in his mouth. "Fascists *manqués*," he said.

Wendell rejected the pipe Beatrice offered him.

"Give it back to our teacher. We need his wisdom. We need the fruit of his suffering."

"*Manqué* see, *manqué* do," Bech went on, puffing and inhaling. What a woman must feel like in coitus. More, more.

"*Mon maître*," Wendell sighed, leaning forward, breathless, awed, loving.

"Suffering," Norma sneered. "The day Henry Bech lets himself suffer is a day I'm dying to see. He's the safest man in America, since they retired Tom Dewey. Oh, this is horrible. You're all being so silly and here I sit perfectly sober. I hate it. I hate *all* of you, absolutely."

"Do you hear music?" Bech asked, passing the pipe directly across to Wendell.

"Look at the windows, everybody people," Beatrice said. "They're coming into the room."

"*Stop* pretending," Norma told her. "You *always* played up to Mother. I'd rather be nobby Norma than bland Bea."

"She's beautiful," Wendell said, to Norma, of Beatrice. "But so are you. The Lord Krishna bestows blessings with a lavish hand."

Norma turned to him and grinned. Her tropism to the phony like a flower's to the sun. Wide warm mouth wherein memories of pleasure have become poisonous words.

Carefully Bech asked the other man, "Why does your face resemble the underside of a colander in which wet lettuce is heaped?" The image seemed both elegant and precise, cruel yet just. But the thought of lettuce troubled his digestion. Grass. All men. Things grow in circles. Stop the circles.

"I sweat easily," Wendell confessed freely. The easy shamelessness purchased for an ingrate generation by decades of poverty and war.

"And write badly," Bech said.

Wendell was unabashed. He said, "You haven't seen my new stuff. It's really terrifically controlled. I'm letting the things dominate the emotions instead of vice versa. Don't you think, since the 'Wake,' emotions have about had it in prose?"

"Talk to *me*," Norma said. "*He's* absolutely self-obsessed."

Wendell told her simply, "He's my god."

Beatrice was asking, "Whose turn is it? Isn't anybody else worried about the windows?" Wendell gave her the pipe. She smoked and said, "It tastes like dregs."

When she offered the pipe to Bech, he gingerly waved it away. He felt that the summit of his apotheosis had slipped by, replaced by a widespread sliding. His perceptions were clear, he felt them all trying to get through to him, Norma seeking love, Wendell praise, Beatrice a few more days of free vacation; but these arrows of demand were directed at an object in metamorphosis. Bech's chest was sloping upward, trying to lift his head into steadiness, as when, thirty years ago, carsick on the long subway ride to his Brooklyn uncles, he would fix his eyes in a death grip on his own reflection in the shuddering black glass. The funny wool Buster Brown cap his

mother made him wear, his pale small face, old for
his age. The ultimate deliverance of the final
stomach-wrenching stop. In the lower edge of his
vision Norma leaped up and grabbed the pipe from
Beatrice. Something fell. Sparks. Both women scrambled on the floor. Norma arose in her shimmering
kimono and majestically complained, "It's out. It's
all gone. Damn you, greedy Bea!"

"Back to Mexico," Bech called. His own voice came
from afar, through blankets of a gathering expect-
ancy, the expanding motionlessness of nausea. But
he did not know for a certainty that he was going
to be sick until Norma's voice, a few feet away in
the sliding obfuscation, as sharp and small as something seen in reversed binoculars, announced,
"Henry, you're absolutely yellow!"

In the bathroom mirror he saw that she was right.
The blood had drained from his long face, leaving
like a scum the tallow of his summer tan, and a
mauve blotch of sunburn on his melancholy nose.
Face he had glimpsed from a thousand pits, in bar-
bershops and barrooms, in subways and airplane
windows above the Black Sea, before shaving and
after lovemaking, it witlessly smiled, the eyes very
tired. Bech kneeled and submitted to the dark
ecstasy of being eclipsed, his brain shouldered into
nothingness by the violence of the inversion
whereby his stomach emptied itself, repeatedly, until a satisfying pain scraped tears from his eyes, and
he was clean.

· · ·

Beatrice sat alone in the living room, beside the dead fireplace. Bech asked her, "Where is everybody?"

She said, unmoving, uncomplaining, "They went outside and about two minutes ago I heard his car motor start."

Bech, shaken but sane, said, "Another medical fact exploded."

Beatrice looked at him questioningly. Flirting her head, Bech thought, like Norma. Sisters. A stick refracted in water. Our biological mother.

He explained, "A, the little bastard tells me it won't make me sick, and B, he solemnly swears it's a sexual depressant."

"You don't think—they went back to his room?"

"Sure. Don't you?"

Beatrice nodded. "That's how she is. That's how she's always been."

Bech looked around him, and saw that the familiar objects—the jar of dried bayberry; the loose shell collections, sandy and ill-smelling; the damp stack of books on the sofa—still wore one final, gossamer thickness of the mystery in which marijuana had clothed them. He asked Bea, "How are you feeling? Do the windows still worry you?"

"I've been sitting here watching them," she said. "I keep thinking they're going to tip and fall into the room, but I guess they won't really."

"They might," Bech told her. "Don't sell your intuitions short."

"Please, could you sit down beside me and watch

them with me? I know it's silly, but it would be a help."

He obeyed, moving Norma's wicker chair close to Bea, and observed that indeed the window frames, painted white in unpainted plank walls, did have the potentiality of animation, and a disturbing pressingness. Their center of gravity seemed to shift from one corner to the other. He discovered he had taken Bea's hand—limp, cool, less bony than Norma's—into his. She gradually turned her head, and he turned his face away, embarrassed that the scent of vomit would be still on his breath. "Let's go outside on the porch," he suggested.

The stars overhead were close and ripe. What was that sentence from *Ulysses?* Bloom and Stephen emerging from the house to urinate, suddenly looking up—*The heaventree of stars hung with humid nightblue fruit.* Bech felt a sadness, a terror, that he had not written it. Not ever. A child whimpered and rustled in its sleep. Beatrice was wearing a loose pale dress luminous in the air of the dark porch. The night was moist, alive; lights along the horizon pulsed. The bell buoy clanged on a noiseless swell. She sat in a chair against the shingled wall and he took a chair facing her, his back to the sea. She asked, "Do you feel betrayed?"

He tried to think, scanned the scattered stars of his decaying brain for the answer. "Somewhat. But I've had it coming to me. I've been getting on her nerves deliberately."

"Like me and Rodney."

He didn't answer, not comprehending and marveling instead how, when the woman crossed and recrossed her legs, it could have been Norma—a gentler, younger Norma.

She clarified, "I forced the divorce."

The child who had whimpered now cried aloud; it was little Donald, pronouncing hollowly, "The owl!"

Beatrice, struggling for control against her body's slowness, rose and went to the child, kneeled and woke him. "No owl," she said. "Just Mommy." With that ancient strange strength of mothers she pulled him from the sleeping bag and carried him back in her arms to her chair. "No owl," she repeated, rocking gently, "just Mommy and Uncle Harry and the bell buoy."

"You smell funny," the child told her.

"Like what funny?"

"Like sort of candy."

"Donald," Bech said, "we'd never eat any candy without telling you. We'd never be so mean."

There was no answer; he was asleep again.

"I admire you," Beatrice said at last, the lulling rocking motion still in her voice, "for being yourself."

"I've tried being other people," Bech said, fending, "but nobody was convinced."

"I love your book," she went on. "I didn't know how to tell you, but I always rather sneered at you, I thought of you as part of Norma's phony crowd, but your writing, it's terribly tender. There's something in you that you keep safe from all of us."

As always when his writing was discussed to his face, a precarious trembling entered Bech's chest. A case of crystal when heavy footsteps pass. He had the usual wild itch to run, to disclaim, to shut his eyes in ecstasy. More, more. He protested, "Why didn't anybody at least knock on the door when I was dying in the bathroom? I haven't whoopsed like that since the army."

"I wanted to, but I couldn't move. Norma said it was just your way of always being the center of attention."

"That bitch. Did she really run off with that woolly little prep-school snot?"

Beatrice said, with an emphatic intonation dimly, thrillingly familiar, "You *are* jealous. You *do* love her."

Bech said, "I just don't like creative-writing students pushing me out of my bed. I make a good Phoenician Sailor but I'm a poor Fisher King."

There was no answer; he sensed she was crying. Desperately changing the subject, he waved toward a distant light, whirling, swollen by the mist. "That whole headland," he said, "is owned by an ex-member of the Communist Party, and he spends all his time putting up No Trespassing signs."

"You're nice," Beatrice sobbed, the child at rest in her arms.

A motor approached down the muffling sandy road. Headlights raked the porch rail, and doubled footsteps crashed through the cottage. Norma and Wendell emerged onto the porch, Wendell carrying a messy thickness of typewriter paper. "Well," Bech said, "that didn't take long. We thought you'd be gone for the night. Or is it dawn?"

"Oh, Henry," Norma said, "you think *every*thing is sex. We went back to Wendell's place to flush his LSD down the toilet, he felt so guilty when you got sick."

"Never again for me, Mr. Bech. I'm out of that subconscious bag. Hey, I brought along a section of my thing, it's not exactly a novel, you don't have to read it now if you don't want to."

"I couldn't," Bech said. "Not if it makes distinctions."

Norma felt the changed atmosphere and accused her sister, "Have you been boring Henry with what an awful person I am? How could the two of you *ima*gine I'd misbe*have* with this *boy* under your noses? Surely I'm subtler than *that*."

Bech said, "We thought you might be high on pot."

Norma triumphantly complained, "I never got *any*thing. And I'm *pos*itive the rest of you faked it." But, when Wendell had been sent home and the children had been tucked into their bunks, she fell asleep with such a tranced soundness that Bech, insomniac, sneaked from her side and safely slept with Beatrice. He found her lying awake waiting for him. By fall the word went out on the literary circuit that Bech had shifted mistresses again.

Bech Panics

THIS MOMENT IN BECH's PILGRIMAGE must be approached reverently, hesitantly, as befits a mystery. We have these few slides: Bech posing before a roomful of well-groomed girls spread seraglio-style on the floor, Bech lying awake in the frilly guest room of a dormitory, Bech conversing beside a granite chapel with a woman in a purple catsuit, Bech throwing himself like a seed upon the leafy sweet earth of Virginia, within a grove of oaks on the edge of the campus, and mutely begging Someone, Something, for mercy. Otherwise, there is semi-darkness, and the oppressive roar of the fan that cools the projector, and the fumbling, snapping noises as the projectionist irritably hunts for slides that are not there. What made Bech panic? That particular March, amid the ripening aromas of rural Virginia, in that lake of worshipful girls?

All winter he had felt uneasy, idle, irritable, displaced. He had broken with Norma and was seeing Bea. The train ride up to Ossining was dreary, and the children seemed, to this bachelor, surprisingly omnipresent; the twin girls sat up watching television until "Uncle Harry" himself was nodding, and then in the heart of the night little Donald would sleepwalk, sobbing, into the bed where Bech lay with his pale, gentle, plump beloved. The first time the child, in blind search of his mother, had touched Bech's hairy body, he had screamed, and in turn Bech had screamed. Though Donald, who had few preconceptions, soon grew adept at sorting out the muddle of flesh he sometimes found in his mother's bed, Bech on his side never quite adjusted to the smooth transition between Bea's lovemaking and her mothering. Her tone of voice, the curve of her gestures, seemed the same. He, Bech, forty-four and internationally famous, and this towheaded male toddler depended parallel from the same broad body, the same silken breasts and belly, the same drowsy croons and intuitive caresses. Of course, abstractly, he knew it to be so—Freud tells us, all love is one, indivisible, like electricity—but concretely this celibate man of letters, who had been an only son and who saw his sister's family in Cincinnati less than once a year, felt offended at his immersion in the ooze of familial promiscuity. It robbed sex of grandeur if, with Bech's spunk still dribbling from her vagina and her startled yips of pleasure still ringing in his dreams, Bea could rouse and turn and almost identically minister to a tot's fit of nightfright.

It made her faintly comical and unappetizing, like the giant milk dispenser in a luncheonette. Sometimes, when she had not bothered to put on her nightie, or had been unable to find where their amorous violence had tossed it, she nestled the boy to sleep against her naked breasts and Bech would find himself curled against her cool backside, puzzled by priorities and discomfited by the untoward development of jealousy's adamant erection.

His attempts to separate her from her family were not successful. Once he stayed at a motel near the railroad station, and took her out, in her own car, on a "date" that was to proceed, after dinner, to his hired room, and was to end with Bea's return home no later than midnight, since the babysitter was the fifteen-year-old daughter of the local Methodist minister. But the overfilling meal at a boorish roadside restaurant, and their furtive decelerated glide through the crackling gravel courtyard of the motel (where a Kiwanis banquet was in progress, and had hogged all the parking spaces), and his fumbly rush to open the tricky aluminoid lock-knob of his door and to stuff his illicit guest out of sight, and the macabre interior of oak-imitating wallboard and framed big-eyed pastels that embowered them proved in sum withering to Bech's potency. Though his suburban mistress graciously, following less her own instincts than the exemplary drift of certain contemporary novels, tried to bring his weakling member to strength by wrapping it in the velvet bandages of her lips, Bech couldn't achieve more than a two-thirds hard-on, which diminished to an even less usable fraction whenever the starchy fare within their stomachs rumbled, or his gaze met that of a pastel waif, or the Kiwanis broke into another salvo of applause, or Bea's beginning yips frightened him up from the primordial level where he was, at last, beginning to thrive. Who, as a rabbi once said, by taking thought can add a cubit to his height? Not Bech, though he tried. The minister's freckle-faced daughter was asleep on the sofa when he and Bea finally returned, as stiff with dried sweat as a pair of squash players.

In Manhattan, on Bech's cozy turf, the problem was different: Bea underwent a disquieting change. At home in Bech's drab large rooms at Riverside and Ninety-ninth, she became slangy, bossy, twitchy, somewhat sluttish, too much at home—she became in short like her rejected sister Norma. The Latchett blood ran tart at the scent of marriage; old Judge Latchett, when alive, had been one of the hanginger magistrates in Jersey City. Bea, as her underwear and Bech's socks dried together on the bathroom radiator, tended to pontificate. "You should get out of these dreary rooms, Henry. They're half the reason you're blocked."

"Am I blocked? I'd just thought of myself as a slow typist."

"What do you do, hit the space bar once a day?"

"Ouch."

"I'm sorry, that did sound bitchy. But it makes

me *sad*, to see someone of your beautiful gifts just stagnating."

"Maybe I have a beautiful gift for stagnation."

"Come live with me."

"What about the neighbors? What about the children?"

"The neighbors don't care. The children love you. Come live with us and see in the spring. You're dying of carbon monoxide down here."

"I'd drown in flesh up there. You pin me down and the others play pile-on."

"Only Donald. And aren't you funny about that? Rodney and I absolutely agreed, a child shouldn't be excluded from *any*thing physical. We thought *noth*ing of being nude in front of them."

"Spare me the picture, it's like a Grünewald. You and Rodney, as I understand it, agreed about everything."

"Well at least neither of us were squeamish old maids."

"Unlike a certain *écrivain juif, n'est-ce pas?*"

"You're very good at making me sound like a bitch. But I honestly *do* believe, Henry, you need to do something different with yourself."

"Such as integrating Suburbia. Henry Bech, Ossining's one-man ghetto."

"It's not like that. It's not like a Polish village. Nobody thinks in these categories any more."

"Will I be asked to join the Kiwanis? Does a mama's lover qualify to join the P.-T.A.?"

"They don't call it the P.-T.A. any more."

"Bea baby, here I stand, I can do no other. I've lived here twenty years."

"That is precisely your problem."

"Every shop on Broadway knows me. From the Chinese laundry to the Swedish bakery. From Fruit House to Japanese Foodland. There he goes, they say, Old Man Bech, a legend in his lifetime. Or, as the colored on the block call me, Cheesecake Charley, the last of the Joe Louis liberals."

"You're really terrified, aren't you," Bea said, "of having a serious conversation?"

The telephone rang. Without the telephone, Bech wondered, how would we ever avoid proposing marriage? The instrument sat by a window, on a table with a chessboard inlaid into veneer warped by years of disuse and steam heat. A dust-drenched shaft of four o'clock sun dwelt tepidly upon a split seam in the sofa cover, a scoop-shaped dent in the lampshade, a yellowing stack of unread presentation copies of once-new novels, arranged to lend stability to the chess table's rickety, dried-out legs. The phone directory was years old and its cover was scrawled with numbers that Bech no longer called, including, in happy crimson greedily inked early one morning, Norma's. The receiver, filmed by air pollution, held a history of fingerprints. "Hello?"

"Mistah Bech? Is that Hainry Bech the authuh?"

"Could be," Bech said. The Southern voice, delightfully female, went on, with a lacy interweave of cajoling and hysterical intonations, to propose that he come and speak or read, whicheveh he

prefuhhed, to a girl's college in Virginia. Bech said,
"I'm sorry, I don't generally do that sort of thing."

"Oh Mistah Bech, Ah *knew* you'd say that, ouah
English instructah, a Miss Eisenbraun, ah don't suppose you know heh, *sayd* you were immensely hard
to gait, but you have *so* many fayuns among the
girls heah, we're all just hopin' against hope."

"Well," Bech said—a bad word choice, in the situation.

The voice must have sensed he found the accent
seductive, for it deepened. "Oueh countrehsaad
round heah is eveh so pretteh, the man who wrote
Travel Laaht owes it to himself to see it, and though
to be shooah we all know moneh is no temptation
foh a man of yoh statchuh, we have a *goood* speak-
eh's budget this ye-ah and kin offeh you—" And she
named a round figure that did give Bech pause.

He asked, "When would this be?"

"Oh!"—her yip was almost coital—"oh, Misteh
Bech, you mean you *maaht?*" Before she let him
hang up he had agreed to appear in Virginia next
month. Bea was indignant. "You've lost all your prin-
ciples. You let yourself be sweet-talked into that."

Bech shrugged. "I'm trying to do something different with myself."

Bea said, "Well I didn't mean letting yourself be
cooed at by an auditorium full of fluffy-headed
racists."

"I think of it more as being an apostle to the Gentiles."

"You won't speak at Columbia when it's two subway stops away and full of people on your own wavelength, but you'll fly a thousand miles to some third-rate finishing school on the remote chance you can sack out with Scarlett O'Hara. You are sick, Henry. You are weak, and sick."

"Actually," Bech told Bea, "I'll be there two nights. So I can sack out with Melanie too."

Bea began to cry. The inner slump he felt, seeing her proud Saxon chin crumple and her blond head bow, was perhaps a premonition of his panic. He tried to joke through it: "Bea baby, I'm just following your orders, I'm going to see spring in in the suburbs. They offered me an even grand. I'll buy a triple bed for you, me, and Donald."

Her blue eyes went milky; her lips and lids became the rubbed pink color of her nipples. She had washed her hair and was wearing only his silk bathrobe, one Norma had given him in response to the gift of a kimono, and when Bea bowed her head and pressed the heels of her hands into her eyes, the lapels parted and her breasts hung lustrous in his sight. He tried to fetch up some words of comfort but knew that none would be comfort enough but the words, "Marry me." So he looked away, past the dented lampshade, at the framed rectangle of city that he knew better than he knew his own soul— the fragile forest of television aerials, the stunted courtyards of leafless ailanthus, the jammed clockwork of fire escapes. His slump hung nervously suspended within him, like a snagged counterweight.

. . .

Two petite, groomed, curried girls met him at the airport and drove him in a pink convertible, at great speed, through the rolling, burgeoning landscape. Spring had arrived here. New York had been windy and raw. The marzipan monuments of Washington, seen from the airport, had glittered above cherry blossoms. Piedmont Air Lines had lifted him and rocked him above hills dull evergreen on the ridges and fresh deciduous green in the valleys, where streams twinkled. The shadow of the plane crossed racetrack ovals and belts of plowed land. Dot-sized horses slowly traced lines of gallop within fenced diagrams. Looking down, Bech was vertiginous; twice they bumped down into small airports cut into hillsides. On the third stop, he alighted. The sun stood midway down the sky, as it had the day the phone had rung and Bea had mocked his acceptance, but now the time stood an hour later in the day; it was after five. The two girls, giggling, gushing, met him and drove him, in a deafening rush of speed (if the convertible flipped, his head would be scraped from his shoulders; he foresaw the fireman hosing his remains from the highway) to a campus, once a great plantation. Here many girls in high heels and sheer stockings and, Bech felt, girdles strolled across acres of hilly lawn overswept by the strong smell of horse manure. In his urban nostrils, the stench rampaged, but nothing in the genteel appearance of the place acknowledged it—not the scrubbed and powdered faces of the girls, nor the brick-and-trim façades of the buildings, nor the

magnolia trees thick and lumpy with mauve-and-
cream, turnip-shaped buds. It was as if one of his
senses had short-circuited to another channel, or as
if a school of deaf-mutes were performing a minuet
to the mistaken accompaniment of a Wagnerian
storm. He felt suddenly, queasily hollow. The de-
clining sun nubbled the lawn's texture with shad-
owed tufts, and as Bech was led along a flagstone
path to his first obligation (an "informal" hour with
the Lanier Club, a branch of budding poetesses)
profound duplicity seemed to underlie the landscape. Along with the sun's reddening rays and the
fecal stench a devastating sadness swept in. He knew
that he was going to die. That his best work was
behind him. That he had no business here, and was
frighteningly far from home.

Bech had never gone to college. War had come
when he was eighteen, and a precocious acceptance
from *Liberty* two years later. He stayed in Germany
a year after V-E Day, editing a newssheet for the
U.S. occupation forces in Berlin, and returned home
to find his father dying. When in time the man—not
even old, merely in his fifties—had surrendered the
last shred of his trachea to the surgeon's knife and
had beat his way back from the underworld of an-
aesthesia for the final time, Bech felt he knew too
much for college. He joined the army of vets who
believed they had earned the right to invent their
lives. He entered a tranced decade of abstract love,
of the exhilarations of type and gossip and nights
spent sitting up waiting for the literary renaissance

that would surely surpass that of the twenties but
just as much as this war had surpassed, in nobility
and breadth and conclusiveness, its predecessor. But
it was there, with the gaunt Titans of modernism,
with Joyce and Eliot and Valéry and Rilke, that one
must begin. *Make it new. The intolerable wrestle
with words and meanings.* Bech weaned himself
from the slicks and wormed his way into the quar-
terlies. *Commentary* let him use a desk. As he confessed to Vera Glavanakova, he wrote poems: thin
poems scattered on the page like soot on snow. He
reviewed books, any books, history, mysteries, al-
manacs, pornography—anything printed had magic.
For some months he was the cinema critic for an
ephemeral journal titled *Displeasure.* Bech was un-
prepossessing then, a scuttler, a petty seducer, a
bright-eyed bug of a man in those days before
whiskey and fame fleshed him out, his head little
more than a nose and a cloud of uncombable hair.
He was busy and idle, melancholy and happy.
Though he rarely crossed the water necessary to
leave Manhattan, he was conscious of freedom—his
freedom to sleep late, to eat ham, to read the
Arabian Nights in the 42nd Street library, to sit an
hour in the Rembrandt room at the Metropolitan,
to chisel those strange early paragraphs, not quite
stories, which look opaque when held in the lap but
held up to the window reveal a symmetrical translucence of intended veins. In the years before
Travel Light, he paced his gray city with a hope
in his heart, the expectation that, if not this day the

next, he would perfectly fuse these stone rectangles around him with the gray rectangles of printed prose. Self-educated, street-educated, then, he was especially vulnerable to the sadness of schools. They stank of country cruelty to him—this herding, this cooping up of people in their animal prime, stunning them with blunt classics, subjecting them to instructors deadened and demented by the torrents of young blood that pass through their years; just the lip-licking reverence with which professors pronounce the word "students" made Bech recoil.

Our slide shows him posturing in a sumptuous common room whose walls are padded with leather-bound editions of Scott and Carlyle and whose floor is carpeted with decorously arranged specimens of nubility. He was, possibly, as charming and witty as usual—the florid letter of thanks he received in New York from the Lanier Club's secretary suggested so. But to himself his tongue seemed to be moving strangely, as slowly as one of those galloping horses he had seen from a mile in the air, while his real attention was turned inward toward the swelling of his dread, his unprecedented recognition of horror. The presences at his feet—those seriously sparkling eyes, those earnestly flushed cheeks, those demurely displayed calves and knees—appalled him with the abyss of their innocence. He felt dizzy, stunned. The essence of matter, he saw, is dread. Death hung behind everything, a real skeleton about to leap through a door in these false walls of books. He saw himself, in this nest of delicate limbs, limbs still ripening toward the wicked seductiveness Nature intended, as a seed among too many eggs, as a gross thrilling intruder, a genuine male intellectual Jew, with hairy armpits and capped molars, a man from the savage North, the North that had once fucked the South so hard it was still trembling—Bech saw himself thus, but as if in a *trompe-l'œil* box whose painted walls counterfeit, from the single perspective of the peephole, three-dimensional furnishings and a succession of archways. He felt what was expected of him, and felt himself performing it, and felt the fakery of the performance, and knew these levels of perception as the shifting sands of absurdity, nullity, death. His death gnawed inside him like a foul parasite while he talked to these charming daughters of fertile Virginia.

One asked him, "Suh, do you feel there is any place left in modern poetry for *rhaam?*"

"For what?" Bech asked, and educed a gale of giggles.

The girl blushed violently, showing blood suddenly as a wound. "For rhy-em," she said. She was a delicate creature, with a small head on a long neck. Her blue eyes behind glasses felt to be on stalks. The sickness in Bech bit deeper as he apologized, "I'm sorry, I simply didn't hear what you said. You ask about rhyme. I write only prose—"

A sweet chorus of mutters protested that No, his prose was a poet's, was poetry.

He went on, stooping with the pain inside him, dazed to hear himself make a kind of sense,

"—but it seems to me rhyme is one of the ways we make things hard for ourselves, make a game out of nothing, so we can win or lose and lighten the, what?, the *indeterminacy* of life. Paul Valéry, somewhere, discusses this, the first line that comes as a gift from the gods and costs nothing, and then the second line that we make ourselves, word by word, straining all our resources, so that it harmonizes with the supernatural first, so that it *rhymes*. He thought, as I remember, that our lives and thoughts and language are all a 'familiar chaos' and that the arbitrary tyranny of a strict prosody goads us to feats of, as it were, rebellion that we couldn't otherwise perform. To this I would only add, and somewhat in contradiction, that rhyme is very ancient, that it marks rhythm, and that much in our natural lives is characterized by rhythm."

"Could you give us an example?" the girl asked.

"For example, lovemaking," Bech said, and to his horror beheld her blush surging up again, and beheld beyond her blush an entire seething universe of brainless breeding, of moist interpenetration, of slippery clinging copulation, of courtship dances and come-on signals, of which her hapless blush, unknown to her, was one. He doubted that he could stand here another minute without fainting. Their massed fertility was overwhelming; their bodies were being broadened and readied to generate from their own cells a new body to be pushed from the old, and in time to push bodies from itself, and so on into eternity, an ocean of doubling and redou-

bling cells within which his own conscious moment
was soon to wink out. He had had no child. He had
spilled his seed upon the ground. Yet we are all seed
spilled upon the ground. These thoughts, as Valéry
had predicated, did not come neatly, in chiming
packets of language, but as slithering, overlapping
sensations, microörganisms of thought setting up in
sum a panicked sweat on Bech's palms and a palpa-
ble nausea behind his belt. He attempted to grin,
and the pond of young ladies shuddered, as if a
pebble had been dropped among them. In rescue
an unseen clock chimed the half-hour, and a ma-
tronly voice, in the accents of Manhattan, called,
"Girls, we must let our guest eat!"

Bech was led to a cathedral-sized dining room
and seated at a table with eight young ladies. A
colored girl sat on his right. She was one of two in
the school. The student body, by its own petition, in
the teeth of parental protests and financial curtail-
ments from the state legislature, had integrated itself. The girl was rather light-skinned, with an Afro
hair-do cut like an upright loaf of bread; she spoke
to Bech in a voice from which all traces of Dixie had
been clipped. "Mr. Bech," she said, "we admire your
gifts of language but wonder if you aren't, now and
then, somewhat racist?"

"Oh? When?" The presence of food—shrimp salad
nested in lettuce, in tulip glasses—had not relieved
his panic; he wondered if he dared eat. The shrimp
seemed to have retained their legs and eyes.

"In *Travel Light*, for example, you keep calling Roxanne a Negress."

"But she was one." He added, "I loved Roxanne."

"The fact is, the word has distinctly racist overtones."

"Well, what should we call them?"

"I suppose you might say 'black women.'" But her primness of tone implied that she, like a spinster lecturing on male anatomy, would rather not call certain things anything at all. Bech was momentarily roused from his funk by this threat, that there were holes in language, things that could not be named. He told her, "Calling you a black woman is as inexact as calling me a pink man."

She responded promptly. "Calling me a Negress is as insulting as calling you a kike."

He liked the way she said it. Flat, firm, clear. Fuck you. Black is beautiful. Forced by the argument to see her color, he saw that her loaf of hair was cinnamon-tinted and a spatter of freckles saddled the bridge of her nose. Through this he saw, in a sliding succession of imagery that dumped him back into terror, an Irish overseer raping a slave, vomiting slaves packed beneath the deck of a bucking ship, Africans selling Africans, tribes of all colors torturing one another, Iroquois thrusting firebrands down the throats of Jesuits, Chinese skinning each other in careful strips, predation and cruelty reaching back past Man to the dawn of life, paramecia in a drop of water, aeons of evolution, each turn of beak or stretch of toe shaped by a geological patter of individual deaths. His words echoed weakly in the deep well of this vision. "A black woman could be a woman who's painted herself black. 'Negro' designates a scientific racial grouping, like Caucasian or Mongolian. I use it without prejudice."

"How do you feel then about 'Jewess'?"

Bech lied; the word made him wince. "Just as I do about 'duchess.'"

"As to your love," the girl went on, still with deliberate dignity, holding her head erect as if balancing something upon it and addressing the entire table in full consciousness of dominating, "we've had enough of your love. You've been loving us down in Georgia and Mississippi for hundreds of years. We've been loved to death, we want now to be respected."

"By which you mean," Bech told her, "you want to be feared."

A white girl at the table broke in with hasty politeness. "Pahdon me, Beth Ann, but Misteh Bech, do you *realleh* believe in races? The school I went to befoh, they made us read a Misteh Carleton Coon? He says, I don't believe a word of it but he says, black folks have longer *heels*, thet's whah the men run fastuh in *sprints?*"

"Black *people*, Cindy," Beth Ann corrected. "Not black 'folks.'" At her prim shudder the ring of pink faces broke into relieved, excessive laughter.

Cindy blushed but was not deflected; she continued, "Also he says, Misteh Bech, that they have thinneh *skulls*, thet's whah so many dah in the prahz ring? We used to be told they had *thick*ehl"

Bech Panics

Puzzled by the intensity of her blush, Bech saw that for this excited young convert to liberalism anthropology was as titillating as pornography. He saw that even in an age of science and unbelief our ideas are dreams, styles, superstitions, mere animal noises intended to repel or attract. He looked around the ring of munching females and saw their bodies as a Martian or a mollusc might see them, as pulpy stalks of bundled nerves oddly pinched to a bud of concentration in the head, a hairy bone knob holding some pounds of jelly in which a trillion circuits, mostly dead, kept records, coded motor operations, and generated an excess of electricity that pressed into the hairless side of the head and leaked through the orifices, in the form of pained, hopeful noises and a simian dance of wrinkles. Impossible mirage! A blot on nothingness. And to think that all the efforts of his life—his preening, his lovemaking, his typing—boiled down to the attempt to displace a few sparks, to bias a few circuits, within some random other scoops of jelly that would, in less time than it takes the Andreas Fault to shrug or the tail-tip star of Scorpio to crawl an inch across the map of Heaven, be utterly dissolved. The widest fame and most enduring excellence shrank to nothing in this perspective. As Bech ate, mechanically offering votive bits of dead lamb to the terror enthroned within him, he saw that the void should have been left unvexed, should have been spared this trouble of matter, of life, and, worst, of consciousness.

· · ·

Slide Two. His bedroom was the corner first-floor room of a large new neo-Georgian dorm. Locked glass doors discreetly separated his quarters from the corridors where virginity slept in rows. But frilly touches whispered and giggled in the room—the beribboned lampshade, the petticoat curtains of dotted swiss beneath the velvet drapes, the abundance of lace runners and china figurines on dainty tables. His bed, with its two plumped pillows one on top of the other like a Pop Art sandwich, its brocaded coverlet turned down along one corner like an Open Here tab on a cereal box, seemed artificially crisp and clean: a hospital bed. And indeed, like an infirm man, he discovered he could lie only in one position, on his back. To turn onto either side was to tip himself toward the edge of a chasm; to roll over onto his belly was to risk drowning in the oblivion that bubbled up from the darkness heated by his own body. The college noises beyond his windows drifted into silence. The last farewell was called, the last high heels tapped down a flagstone path. Chapel bells tolled the quarter hours. The land beyond the campus made itself heard in the sounds of a freight train, an owl, a horse faintly whinnying in some midnight meadow where manure and grass played yin and yang. Bech tried concentrating on these noises, pressing from them, by sheer force of attention, the balm of their undeniability, the innocence that somehow characterized their simple existence, apart from their attributes. All things have the same existence, share the same atoms, reshuffled: grass into manure,

flesh into worms. A blackness beneath this thought
like glass from which frost is rubbed. He tried to
relive pleasantly his evening triumph, his so warmly
applauded reading: he had read a long section from
Brother Pig, the part where the hero rapes his step-
daughter in the bowling alley, behind the pin-setting
machine, and had been amazed, as he read, by the
coherence of the words, by their fearless onward
march. The blanket of applause, remembered, op-
pressed him. He tried word games. He went through
the alphabet with world saviors: Attila, Buddha,
Christ, Danton . . . Woodrow Wilson, Xerxes the
Great, Brigham Young, Zoroaster. There was some
slight comfort in the realization that the world had
survived all its saviors, but Bech had not put himself
to sleep. His panic, like a pain which intensifies when
we dwell upon it, when we inflame it with undivided
attention, felt worse away from the wash of applause; yet, like a wound tentatively defined by the
body's efforts of asepsis and rejection, it was revealing a certain shape. It felt pasty and stiff. Mixed with
the fear, a kind of coagulant, was shame: shame at
his having a "religious crisis" that, by all standard
psychology, should have been digested in early
adolescence, along with post-masturbatory guilt;
shame at the degradation of a one-time disciple of
those great secreters Flaubert and Joyce into a slick
crowd-pleaser at whistle-stop colleges; shame at having argued with a Negress, at having made Bea cry,
at having proved himself, in his relations with all
women from his mother on, a thin-skinned, fastidi-

ous, skittish, slyly clowning cold-blooded ingrate.
Now that she was too anginal and arthritic to live
alone, he had stuck his mother into a Riverdale nursing home, instead of inviting her into his own spa-
cious rooms, site of his dreary, sterile privacy. His
father, in his position, would have become his mother's nurse. His grandfather would have become her
slave. Six thousand years of clan loyalty were overturned in Bech. He denied even his characters the
final measure of love, that would enable them to
break free of his favorite tropes, the ruts of his
phrases, the chains that rattled whenever he sat
down at the typewriter. He tried to analyze himself.
He reasoned that since the id cannot entertain the
concept of death, which by being not-being is nothing to be afraid of, his fear must be of something
narrower, more pointed and printed. He was afraid
that his critics were right. That his works were indeed flimsy, unfelt, flashy, and centrifugal. That the
proper penance for his artistic sins was silence and
reduction; that his id, in collaboration with the su-
perego figures of Alfred Kazin and Dwight Macdonald, had successfully reduced him to artistic
impotence and was now seeking, in its rambling,
large-hearted way, his personal extinction: hence his
pipsqueak ego's present flutter of protest. As soon
sleep in a cement mixer as amid these revelations.
Sleep, the foreshadow of death, the dab of poison we
daily take to forestall convulsion, became impossible.
The only position in which Bech could even half-
relax was on his back, his head propped on both

pillows to hold him above smothering, his limbs held
steady in the fantasy that he was a china figurine,
fragile, cool, and miniature, cupped in a massive
hand. Thus Bech tricked himself, a moment after the
chapel bells had struck three, into sleep—itself a devastating testimony to the body's power to drag us
down with it. His dreams, strange to report, were
light as feathers, and blew this way and that. In one
of them, he talked fluid French with Paul Valéry,
who looked like the late Mischa Auer.

He awoke stiff. He moved from bed to suitcase to
bathroom with an old man's self-dramatizing crouch.
By the light of this new day, through the murky lens
of his panic, objects—objects, those atomic mirages
with edges that hurt—appeared mock-heroic in their
persistence, their quixotic loyalty to the shapes in
which chance has cast them. They seemed to be
watching him, to be animated by their witness of his
plight. Thus, like primitive Man, he began to person-
ify the universe. He shat plenteously, hot gaseous
stuff acidified into diarrhoea, he supposed, by his
fear. He reflected how, these last unproductive years,
his output of excrement had grown so that instead of
an efficient five minutes he seemed to spend most of
his work morning trapped on the toilet, leafing sadly
through *Commentary* and *Encounter*. Elimination
had become Bech's forte: he answered letters with
the promptness of a backboard, he mailed his loose-
paper files to the Library of Congress twice a year.
He had become a compulsive wastebasket-emptier.
Toilets, mailboxes, cunts were all the receptacles of

a fanatic and incessant attempt to lighten himself, as if to fly. Standing at the basin of lavender porcelain (which, newly installed, boasted one of those single faucet controls that blends hot and cold like a joy stick on the old biplanes) Bech, far from his figurine fantasy of last night, felt precariously tall: a sky-high prodigy about to topple, or crumple. His self-ministrations—brushing his teeth, wiping his anus, shaving his jaw—seemed laid upon his body from a cosmic distance, amid the held breath of inert artifacts, frozen presences he believed were wishing him well. He was especially encouraged, and touched, by the elfin bar of motel-size mauve soap his fingers unwrapped across an interstellar gap.

But stepping, dressed, into the sunshine, Bech was crushed by the heedless scale of outdoors. He was overwhelmed by the multiple transparent signs— the buds, the twittering, the springtide glisten—of growth and natural process, the inhuman mutual consumption that is Nature. A zephyr stained by manure recalled his first flash of terror. He ate breakfast stunned, with a tickling in his nose that might have been the wish to cry. Yet the eight girls seated with him—eight new ones, all Caucasian—pretended to find his responses adequate, even amusing. As he was being led to his first display case of the day, a seminar in the postwar American novel, a *zoftig* woman in a purple catsuit accosted him by the chapel. She was lithe, rather short, in her thirties, with brushed-back black hair of which some strands kept drifting onto her temple and cheeks and needed to be brushed back with her fingers, which she did lithely, cleverly, continuously. Her lips were long; the upper bore a faint mustache. Her nose too was long, with something hearteningly developed and intelligent about the modulations from tip to nostril wing. When she spoke, it was not with a Southern accent but with Bech's own, the graceless but rapid and obligingly enunciating accent of New York. She was Jewish.

She said, "Mr. Bech, I know you're being rushed to some important destination, but my girls, the girls you spoke to last night, the Lanier Club, were so, I guess the word is impressed, that they cooked up a rather impertinent, not to say importunate, request that none of them had the nerve to deliver. So they asked me to. I'm their adviser. I was impressed, too, by the way. The name is Ruth Eisenbraun." She offered her hand.

Bech accepted the offer. Her hand was warmer than porcelain, yet exact, and firm. He asked, "What are you doing amid all this alien corn, Ruth?"

The woman said, "Don't knock it, it's a living. This is my fourth year, actually. I like it here. The girls are immensely sweet, and not all of them are dumb. It's a place where you can see things happening, you can actually *see* these kids loosening up. Your consenting to come down here is a tremendous boost to the cause." She took her hand back from his to make the gestures needed to dramatize "loosening up" and "tremendous." In the sunshine glare reflected from the granite chapel Bech could ad-

mire the nimble and even flow of her expressiveness; he enjoyed the sensation, as of a tailor's measurements, of her coolly sizing him up even as she
maintained a screen of patter, every dry and rapid
turn of phrase a calibrated, unembarrassed offer of
herself. "In fact," she was saying, "the society as a
whole is loosening up. If I were a black, the South
is where I'd prefer to be. Nobody in the North believes now in integration because they've never had
it, but here, in an economic and social way, they've
had integration all along, though of course entirely
on the Man's terms. My girls, at least until they
marry the local sheriff or Coke distributor, are really
very naïvely"—again, arabesques with her hands—
"sincerely excited about the idea that black people
are *people*. I find them sweet. After five years at
CCNY, this has been a gigantic breath of fresh air.
You can honestly tell yourself you're *teach*ing these
girls." And by repeating "girls" so often, she was
burning into Bech's fogged brain awareness that she,
something of a girl herself, was also something more.

"What did they want to ask me?"

"Oh, yes. And that seminar is waiting. You know
what their nickname for it is?—'Bellow's Belles.' Now
that's been turned into 'Bellow's Balls.' Isn't that a
good sign, that they can be obscene? *My* girls delegated me to ask *you*"—and Bech inwardly questioned the source of that delegation—"if you'd
please, please, *pret*ty please be willing to judge a
poetry contest of theirs. I got your schedule from
Dean Coates and see you have a big empty slot late

this afternoon; if you could *possibly* make it over to Ruffin Hall at five, they will recite for you in their best Sunday School manner some awful doggerel you can take back to your room, and give us the verdict before you go tomorrow. It is an imposition, I know. I know, I know. But they'll be so thrilled they'll *melt*."

The zipper of her catsuit was open three inches below the base of her throat. If he pulled the zipper down six inches more, Bech estimated, he would discover that she was wearing no bra. Not to mention no girdle. "I'd be pleased to," he said. "Honored, you can tell them."

"God, that's swell of you," Miss Eisenbraun responded briskly. "I hope you weren't hoping to have a nap this afternoon."

"In fact," he told her, "I didn't get much sleep. I feel very strange."

"In what way strange?" She looked up into his face like a dentist who had asked him to open his mouth. She was interested. If he had said hemorrhoids, she would still be interested. Part mother, part clinician. He should have more to do with Jewish women.

"I can't describe it. *Angst*. I'm afraid of dying. Everything is so implacable. Maybe it's all these earth-smells so suddenly."

She smiled and deeply inhaled. When she sniffed, her upper lip broadened, furry. The forgotten downiness of Jewish women. Their hairy thighs. "It's

137

worst in spring," she said. "You get acclimated. May
I ask, have you ever been in analysis?"

His escort of virgins, which had discreetly with-
drawn several yards when Miss Eisenbraun had
pulled her ambush, rustled nervously. Bech bowed.
"I am awaited." Trying to rise to jauntiness from in
under her implication that he was mad, he added,
"See you later, alligator."

"In a while, crocodile": streetcorner yids yukking
it up in the land of milk and honey, giving the gentle
indigines something to giggle about. But with her he
had been able to ignore, for an absent-minded
moment, the gnawing of the worm inside.

How strange, really, his condition was! As absorb-
ing as pain, yet painless. As world-transforming as
drunkenness, yet with no horizon of sobriety. As
debilitating, inwardly, as a severed spine yet per-
mitting him, outwardly, a convincing version of his
usual performance. Which demonstrated, if demonstration were needed, how much of a performance it was. Who was he? A Jew, a modern man,
a writer, a bachelor, a loner, a loss. A con artist in
the days of academic modernism undergoing a Victorian shudder. A white monkey hung far out on a
spindly heaventree of stars. A fleck of dust condemned to know it is a fleck of dust. A mouse in a
furnace. A smothered scream.

His fear, like a fever or deep humiliation, bared
the beauty veiled by things. His dead eyes, cleansed
of healthy egotism, discovered a startled tenderness,
like a virgin's whisper, in every twig, cloud, brick,

pebble, shoe, ankle, window mullion, and bottle-
glass tint of distant hill. Bech had moved, in this
compressed religious evolution of his, from the morning's raw animism to an afternoon of natural romanticism, of pantheistic pangs. Between lunch
(creamed asparagus, French fries, and meatloaf)
and the poetry contest he was free; he took a long
solitary walk around the edges of the campus, inhaling the strenuous odors, being witness to myriad
thrusts of new growth through the woodland's floor
of mulching leaves. Life chasing its own tail. Bech
lifted his eyes to the ridges receding from green to
blue, and the grandeur of the theatre in which Nature stages its imbecile cycle struck him afresh and
enlarged the sore accretion of fear he carried inside
him as unlodgeably as an elastic young wife carries
within her womb her first fruit. He felt increasingly
hopeless; he could never be delivered of this. In a
secluded, sloping patch of oaks, he threw himself
with a grunt of decision onto the damp earth, and
begged Someone, Something, for mercy. He had
created God. And now the silence of the created
universe acquired for Bech a miraculous quality of
willed reserve, of divine tact that would let him
abjectly pray on a patch of mud and make no answer but the familiar ones of rustle, of whisper, of
invisible growth like a net sinking slowly deeper
into the sea of the sky; of gradual realization that
the earth is populated infinitely, that a slithering
slug was slowly causing a dead oak leaf to lift and a

research team of red ants were industriously testing a sudden morsel, Bech's thumb, descended incarnate.

Eventually the author arose and tried to brush the dirt from his knees and elbows. To his fear, and shame, was added anger, anger at the universe for having extracted prayer from him. Yet his head felt lighter; he walked to Ruffin Hall in the mood of a condemned spy who, entering the courtyard where the firing squad waits, at least leaves behind his dank cell. When the girls read their poetry, each word hit him like a bullet. The girl with the small head and the long neck read:

> Air, that transparent fire
> our red earth burns
> as we daily expire,
> sing! As water in urns
> whispers of rivers and wharves,
> sing, life, within the jar
> each warm soul carves
> from this cold star.

There was more to this poem, about Nature, about fine-veined leaves and twigs sharp as bird feet, and more poems, concerning meadows and horses and Panlike apparitions that Bech took to be college boys with sticks of pot, and then more poets, a heavy mannish girl with an unfortunate way of rolling her lips after each long Roethkësque line, and a nun-pale child who indicted our bombing of thatched villages with Lowellian ruminations, and a budding Tallulah swayed equally by Allan Ginsburg and Edna St. Vincent Millay; but Bech's ears closed, his scraped heart flinched. These youthful hearts, he saw, knew all that he knew, but as one knows the rules of a game there is no obligation to play; the sealed structure of naturalism was a school to them, a prison to him. In conclusion, a splendid, goggle-eyed beauty incanted some Lanier, from "The Marshes of Glynn," the great hymn that begins

As the marsh-hen secretly builds on the watery sod,
Behold I will build me a nest on the greatness of God:

and goes on

And the sea lends large, as the marsh: lo, out of his
*   plenty the sea*
Pours fast: full soon the time of the flood-tide must
*   be:*

and ends

The tide is in his ecstasy.
The tide is at his highest height:
And it is night.

Something filmed Bech's eyes, less full-formed tears than the blurry reaction pollen excites in the allergic.

After the poetry reading, there was supper at Madame President's—you know her: hydrangea hair and sweeping manners and a listening smile as keen and neat as an ivory comb. And then there was a symposium, with three students and two members of the English faculty and Bech himself, on "The Destiny of the Novel in a Non-Linear Future." And then a party at the home of the chairman of the department, a bluff old Chaucerian with a flesh-colored hearing aid tucked behind his ear like a wad of chewing gum. The guests came up and performed obeisances, jocular or grave, to Bech, their distinguished interloper, and then resumed seething among each other in the fraught patterns of rivalry and erotic attraction that prevail in English departments everywhere. Amid them Bech felt slow-witted and paunchy; writers are not scholars but athletes, who grow beerbellies after thirty. Miss Eisenbraun detached herself and walked him back across the campus. A fat Southern moon rode above the magnolias and the cupolas.

"You were wonderful tonight," she told him.

"Oh?" Bech said. "I found myself very lumpish."

"You're just marvelously kind to children and bores," she pursued.

"Yes. Fascinating adults are where I fall down."

A little pause, three footsteps' worth, as if to measure the depth of the transaction they were contemplating. One, two, three: a moderate reading. Yet to lift them back over the sill of silence into conversation, a self-conscious effort, something kept in a felt-lined drawer, was needed. She pulled out French.

"*Votre malaise—est-il passé?*" The language of diplomacy.

"*Il passe, mais trés lentement,*" Bech said. "It's becoming part of me."

"Maybe your room has depressed you. Their guest accommodations are terribly little-girly and sterile."

"Exactly. Sterile. I feel I'm an infection. I'm the only germ in a porcelain universe."

She laughed, uncertain. They had reached the glass doors of the dormitory where he slept. An owl hooted. The moon frosted with silver a distant ridge. He wondered if in his room his fear would make him pray again. A muffled radio somewhere played country rock.

"Don't worry," he reassured her. "I'm not catching."

Her laugh changed quality; it became an upwards offer of her throat, followed by her breasts, her body. She was not wearing the catsuit but a black cocktail dress with a square neckline, yet the effect was the same, of a loose slipperiness about her that invited a peeling. She was holding to her breasts a manilla envelope full of poems awaiting his verdict. "I think your room is underfurnished," she told him.

"My rooms in New York are too."

"You need something to sleep beside."

"An oxygen tent?"

"Me."

Bech said, "I don't think we should," and cried. He seemed to mean, to himself, that he was too hideous, too sick; yet also in his mind was the superstition that they must not defile the sleeping dormitory, this halcyon Lesbos, with copulation. Ruth

Eisenbraun stared amazed, her hands tightening on the envelope of poems, at the moonlight making ice of Bech's impotent tears. Her firm willing body, silhouetted against the dewy smell of sleeping grass, seemed to him another poem abysmal in its ignorance, deceitful in its desire to mitigate the universe. Poetry and love, twin attempts to make the best of a bad job. Impotent; yet in his stance, his refusal to embrace, we must admire a type of rigidity, an erect pride in his desolation, a determination to defend it as his territory. A craven pagan this morning, he had become by midnight a stern monk.

This is all speculation. Truly we are in the dark here. Knowing Bech on other, better lit occasions, we doubt that, given this importunate woman, the proximity of the glass doors, and the key in his pocket, he did not for all his infirmity take her inside to his sickbed and let her apply to his wound the humid poultice of her flesh. Also, on her side, Ruth was a professor of literature; she would not have misread the works so badly as to misjudge the man. Picture them then. Above Bech and Ruth hangs the black dome of their sepulchre; the nipples of her breasts also appear black, as they swing above him, teasing his mouth, his mouth blind as a baby's, though his eyes, when he shuts them, see through the succulent padding to the calcium xylophone of her rib cage. His phallus a counterfeit bone, a phantasmal creature, like Man, on the borderline of substance and illusion, of death and life. They establish a rhythm. Her socket becomes a positive force, begins to suck, to pound. Enough. Like Bech, we reach a point where words seem horrible, maggots on the carcass of reality, feeding, proliferating; we seek peace in silence and reduction.

Wait, wait. Here is another slide, a fifth, found hiding under a stack of gold domes from Russia. It shows Bech the next morning. Again, he has slept on his back, his head held high by two pillows, a china figurine through which dreams idly blow. The pillows having been piled one on top of the other prevent our knowing whether or not two heads lay down on the bed. He rises grudgingly, stiffly. Again, he is wonderfully productive of excrement. His wound feels scabbier, drier; he knows now he can get through a day with it, can live with it. He performs his toilet—washes, wipes, brushes, shaves. He sits down at the little pseudo-Sheraton desk and shuffles the sheaf of poems as if they are physically hot. He awards the first prize, a check for $25, to the girl with the small head and blue eyes on stalks, writing as his citation:

Miss Haynsworth's poems strike me as technically accomplished, making their way as good loyal citizens under the tyranny of rhyme, and as precociously rich in those qualities we associate with poetesses from Sappho on—they are laconic, clear-eyed, gracious toward the world, and in their acceptance of our perishing frailty, downright brave.

Bech arranged to have the envelope delivered to Miss Eisenbraun by someone else, and was driven to the airport by a homely, tall, long-toothed woman whose voice, he realized, was the voice that beguiled him over the telephone. "Ah'm *so* sorreh, Misteh Bech, evrehbodeh saiys you were *dahl*in, but Ah had to attend mah sisteh's weddin in Roanoke, it was one of those sudden affaihs, and jes got back this mawnin! Believe me, suh, Ah am *moht*ifahd!"

"Neveh you mind," Bech told her, and touched his inside breast pocket to make sure his check was in it. The landscape, unwinding in reverse, seemed greener than when he arrived, and their speed less dangerous. Bea, who with much inconvenience had hired a babysitter so she could meet him at La Guardia, sensed, just seeing him emerge from the giant silver belly and scuttle across the tarmac in the rain, that something had happened to him, that there wasn't enough of him left for her to have any.

Bech Swings?

Bech arrived in London with the daffodils; he knew that he must fall in love. It was not his body that demanded it, but his art. His first novel, *Travel Light*, had become a minor classic of the fifties, along with *Picnic*, *The Search for Bridey Murphy*, and the sayings of John Foster Dulles. His second novel, a lyrical gesture of disgust, novella-length, called *Brother Pig*, did his reputation no harm and cleared his brain, he thought, for a frontal assault on the wonder of life. The assault, surprisingly, consumed five years, in which his mind and work habits developed in circles, or loops, increasingly leisurely and whimsical; when he sat down at his desk, for instance, his younger self, the somehow fictitious author of his earlier fictions, seemed to be not quite displaced, so that he became an uneasy, blurred composite, like the image left on film by too slow an exposure. The final fruit of his distracted struggles,

147

The Chosen, was universally judged a failure—one of those "honorable" failures, however, that rather endear a writer to the race of critics, who would rather be reassured of art's noble difficulty than cope with a potent creative verve. Bech felt himself rise from the rubble of bad reviews bigger than ever, better known and in greater demand. Just as the id, according to Freud, fails to distinguish between a wish-image and a real external object, so does publicity, another voracious idiot, dismiss all qualitative distinctions and feast off good and bad alike. Now five—no, six—years had passed, and Bech had done little but pose as himself, and scribble reviews and "impressionistic" journalism for *Commentary* and *Esquire,* and design a series of repellent rubber stamps.

> **HENRY BECH REGRETS THAT HE DOES NOT SPEAK IN PUBLIC.**
>
> **SORRY, PETITIONS AREN'T MY METIER.**
>
> **HENRY BECH IS TOO OLD AND ILL AND DOUBTFUL TO SUBMIT TO QUESTIONNAIRES AND INTERVIEWS.**
>
> **IT'S YOUR PH.D. THESIS; PLEASE WRITE IT YOURSELF.**

By appropriately stamping the letters he received and returning them to the sender, Bech simplified his correspondence. But six years had passed, and his third stamp pad had gone dry, and the age of fifty was in sight, and it was high time to write something to justify his sense of himself as a precious and useful recluse. A stimulus seemed needed.

Love? Travel? As to love, he had been recently processed by a pair of sisters, first the one, and then the other; the one was neurotic and angular and harsh and glamorous and childless and exhausting, and the other had been sane and soft and plain and maternal and exhausting. Both had wanted husbands. Both had mundane, utilitarian conceptions of themselves that Bech could not bring himself to corroborate. It was his charm and delusion to see women as deities—idols whose jewel was set not in the center of their foreheads but between their legs, with another between their lips, and pairs more sprinkled up and down, from ankles to eyes, the length of their adorable, alien forms. His transactions with these supernatural creatures imbued him, more keenly each time, with his own mortality. His life seemed increasingly like that sinister fairy story in which each granted wish diminishes a magic pelt that is in fact the wisher's life. But perhaps, Bech thought, one more woman, one more leap would bring him safe into that high calm pool of immortality where Proust and Hawthorne and Catullus float, glassy-eyed and belly up. One more wasting love would release his genius from the bondage of his sagging flesh.

As to travel: his English publisher, J. J. Goldschmidt, Ltd., who had sidestepped Bech's collected essays (published in the United States and Canada as *When the Saints*) and had remaindered *Brother*

Pig with the haste usually reserved for bishops'
memoirs and albums of Pharaonic art, now, possibly
embarrassed by the little novel's creeping success in
its Penguin edition, and guilty over the minuscule
advances and scrimped printings with which he had
bound Bech's thriving name, decided to bring out
a thirty-shilling anthology called, all too inevitably,
The Best of Bech. To support this enterprise he
asked the author to come to London for the week
before publication and permit himself to "be lion-
ized." The phrase snaked in less time than an eye-
blink along three thousand miles of underwater
cable.

"I'd rather be lambified," Bech answered.

"What, Henry? Sorry, I can hardly hear you."

"Forget it, Goldy. It was a hard word."

"You heard what?"

"Nothing. This is a very wet connection."

"Dead?"

"Not yet, but let's kill it. I'll come." He arrived
with the daffodils. The Viscount banked over Hampton Court, and the tinge of their yellow was visible
from the air. In Hyde Park beside the Serpentine,
along Birdcage Walk in St. James's, in Grosvenor
Square beneath the statue of Roosevelt and in Russell Square beneath the statue of Gandhi, in all the
fenced squares from Fitzroy to Pembroke, the daffodils made a million golden curtseys to those tourists
who, like our hero, wandered dazed by jet-lag and
lonely as a cloud. *A poet could not but be gay,* Bech
recalled, *In such a jocund company.* And the people

in the streets, it seemed to him, whether milling along Oxford Street or sauntering from lion to lion in Trafalgar Square, formed another golden host, beautiful in the antique cold-faced way of Blake's pastel throngs, pale Dionysiacs, bare thighs and gaudy cloth, lank hair and bell-bottoms, *Continuous as the stars that shine / And twinkle on the milky way.* And, the next morning, watching Merissa move nude to the window and to her closet, he felt her perfections—the parallel tendons at the back of her knees, the kisslike leaps of shadow among the muscles of her shoulders—flow outdoors and merge with the lacy gauze of the gray British air. A Viscount hung in silent descent above the treetops of Regent's Park. He rose and saw that this park too had its pools of gold, its wandering beds of daffodils, and that under the sunless noon sky lovers, their heads androgynous masses of hair, had come to lie entwined on the cold greening grass. *Cold greening grass,* Bech heard. The echo disturbed and distracted him. The papery daytime world, cluttered with books he had not written, cut into the substantial dreams of drunkenness and love.

Jørgen Josiah Goldschmidt, a bustling small anxious man with an ambitiously large head and the pendulous profile of a Florentine banker, had arranged a party for Bech the very evening of his arrival. "But, Goldy, by your time I've been awake since two this morning."

They had met several times in New York. Goldschmidt had evidently sized up Bech as a clowner
to be chuckled and shushed into line. In turn Bech
had sized up Goldschmidt as one of those self-made
men who have paid the price (for not letting God
make them) of minor defects like inner deafness and
constant neuralgia. Goldschmidt's was a success
story. A Danish Jew, he had arrived in England in
the late thirties. In twenty years, he had gone from
the Ministry of Information to the B.B.C. to an editorship in a venerable publishing house to the
founding, in the mid-fifties, of one of his own, spe-
cializing in foreign avant-garde writers no one else
wanted and dainty anthologies of poetic matter
lapsed from copyright. A lucky recipe book (health
food soups) and a compendium of Prayers for Hu-
manists staved off bankruptcy. Now he was prosperous, thanks mostly to his powers of persuading his
lawyers and printers to let him publish increasingly
obscene American authors. Though devoid of any
personal taste for obscenity, he had found a wave
and was riding it. His accent and dress were im-
peccably British. In tune with the times he had
sprouted bushy sideburns. His face was always
edged with the gray of nagging pain. He said, his
brown eyes (in repose, they revealed lovely amber
depths, lit by the fire of his brain, but were rarely
in repose) flicking past Bech's shoulder toward the
next problem, "Henry, you must come. Everyone is
dying to meet you. I've invited just the very dearest
nicest people. Ted Heath might drop in later, and

Princess Margaret was so sorry she must be in Ceylon. You can have a nice nap in your hotel. If you don't like the room, we can change it. I thought from your books you would enjoy a view of the traffic. Your interview isn't until five, a terribly nice intelligent boy, a compatriot of yours. If you don't like him, just give him a half hour of the usual and he'll be on his way."

Bech protested, "I have no usual," but the other man said deafly, "Bless you," and left.

Too excited by the new city, and by having survived another airplane flight, Bech instead of sleeping walked miles looking at the daffodils, at the Georgian rows plastered with demolition notices and peace slogans, at the ruffled shirts and Unisex pants in the shop windows, at the bobbies resembling humorless male models, at the dingy band of hippies sharing Eros's black island in Piccadilly Circus with pigeons the color of exhaust fumes. On Great Russell Street, down from the British Museum, past a Hindu luncheonette, a plaque marked the site of a Dickens novel as if the characters had occupied the same time-space in which Bech walked. Back in his hotel lobby, he was offended by the American voices, the pseudo-Edwardian decor, the illustrated chart of acceptable credit cards. A typical Goldschmidt snap decision, to stuff him into a tourist trap. A pale young man, plainly American from his round-headed haircut and his clever hangdog way of sidling forward, came up to Bech. "My name is Tuttle, Mr. Bech. I guess I'm going to interview you."

"Your guess is as good as mine," Bech said.

The boy tipped his head slightly, like a radar dish, as if to decipher the something acerb in Bech's tone, and said, "I don't generally do this sort of thing, actually I have as low an opinion of interviews as you do—"

"How do you know I have a low opinion?" Jet-lag was getting to Bech; irritability was droning in his ears.

"You've said so"—the boy smiled shyly, cleverly—"in your other interviews." He went on hastily, pursuing his advantage. "But this wouldn't be like your others. It would be all you, I have no ax to grind, no ax at all. A friend of mine on the staff of the Sunday *Observer* begged me to do it, actually I'm in London researching a thesis on eighteenth-century printers. It would be a sort of full spread to go with *The Best of Bech*. Let me frankly confess, it seemed a unique opportunity. I've written you letters in the past, in the States, but I suppose you've forgotten."

"Did I answer them?"

"You hit them with a rubber stamp and sent them back." Tuttle waited, perhaps for an apology, then went on. "What I have in mind now is a chance for you to explain yourself, to say everything you want to say. *You* want to say. Your *name* is known over here, Mr. Bech, but they don't really know *you*."

"Well, that's their privilege."

"I beg your pardon, sir, I think it's their loss."

Bech felt himself slippingly, helplessly relenting. "Let's sit over here," he said. To take the boy up

154

to his room would, he thought groggily, simulate pederasty and risk the fate of Wilde.

They sat in facing lobby chairs; Tuttle perched on the edge of his as if he had been called into the principal's office. "I've read every word you've written five or six times. Frankly, I think you're *it*." This sounded to Bech like the safest praise he had ever heard; one appetite that had not diminished with the years was for unambiguous, blood-raw superlatives.

He reached over and tagged the boy. "Now you're it," he said.

Tuttle blushed. "I mean to say, what other people *say* they're doing, you really *do*." An echo troubled Bech; he had heard this before, but not applied to himself. Still, the droning had ceased. The blush had testified to some inner conflict, and Bech could maintain his defenses only in the face of a perfectly simple, resolute attack. Any sign of embarrassment or self-doubt he confused with surrender.

"Let's have a drink," he said.

"Thank you, no."

"You mean you're on duty?"

"No, I just don't ever drink."

"Never?"

"No."

Bech thought, They've sent me a Christer. That's what Tuttle's pallor, his sidling severity, his embarrassed insistence reminded Bech of: the Pentecostal fanatic who comes to the door. "Well, let me frankly confess, I sometimes do. Drink."

"Oh, I know. Your drinking is famous."

"Like Hitler's vegetarianism."

In his haste to put Bech at ease, Tuttle neglected to laugh. "Please go ahead," the boy insisted. "If you become incoherent, I'll just stop taking notes, and we can resume another day."

Poor Henry Bech, to whom innocence, in its galoshes of rudeness and wet raincoat of presumption, must always appear as possibly an angel to be sheltered and fed. He ordered a drink ("Do you know what a whiskey sour is?" he asked the waiter, who said "Absolutely, sir" and brought him a whiskey-and-soda) and tried for one more degrading time to dig into the rubbish of his "career" and come up with the lost wristwatch of truth. Encouraged by the fanatic way the boy covered page after page of his notebook with wildly oscillating lines, Bech talked of fiction as an equivalent of reality, and described how the point of it, the justification, seemed to lie in those moments when a set of successive images locked and then one more image arrived and, as it were, superlocked, creating a tightness perhaps equivalent to the terribly tight knit of reality, e.g., the lightning ladder of chemical changes in the body cell that translates fear into action or, say, the implosion of mathematics consuming the heart of a star. And the down-grinding thing is the realization that no one, not critics or readers, ever notices these moments but instead prattles, in praise or blame, of bits of themselves glimpsed in the work as in a shattered mirror. That it is necessary

156

to begin by believing in an ideal reader and that slowly he is proved not to exist. He is not the daily reviewer skimming a plastic-bound set of raggedy advance proofs, nor the bulk-loving housewife who buys a shiny new novel between the grocer's and the hairdresser's, nor the diligent graduate student with his heap of index cards and Xerox applications, nor the plump-scripted young ballpointer who sends a mash note via *Who's Who,* nor, in the weary end, even oneself. In short, one loses heart in the discovery that one is not being read. That the ability to read, and therefore to write, is being lost, along with the abilities to listen, to see, to smell, and to breathe. That all the windows of the spirit are being nailed shut. Here Bech gasped for air, to dramatize his point. He said, then, that he was sustained, insofar as he was sustained, by the memory of laughter, the specifically Jewish, embattled, religious, sufficiently desperate, not quite belly laughter of his father and his father's brothers, his beloved Brooklyn uncles; that the American Jews had kept the secret of this laughter a generation longer than the Gentiles, hence their present domination of the literary world; that unless the Negroes learned to write there was nowhere else it could come from; and that in the world today only the Russians still had it, the Peruvians possibly, and Mao Tse-tung but not any of the rest of the Chinese. In his, Bech's, considered judgment.

Tuttle scribbled another page and looked up hopefully. "Maoism does seem to be the coming mood," he said.

"The mood of t'mao," Bech said, rising. "Believe it or not, my lad, I must take a shower and go to a party. Power corrupts."

"When could we resume? I think we've made a fascinating beginning."

"Beginning? You want *more*? For just a little puff in the *Observer*?"

When Tuttle stood, though he was skinny, with a round head like a newel knob, he was taller than Bech. He got tough. "I want it to be much more than that, Mr. Bech. Much more than a little puff. They've promised me as much space as we need. You have a chance here, if you *use* me hard enough, to made a d-definitive t-t-testament."

If the boy hadn't stammered, Bech might have escaped. But the stammer, those little spurts of helpless silence, hooked him. Stalling, he asked, "You never drink?"

"Not really."

"Do you smoke?"

"No."

"Matter of principle?"

"I just never acquired the taste."

"Do you eat between meals?"

"I guess once in a while."

"Call me tomorrow," Bech conceded, and hated himself. Strange, how dirty the attempt to speak seriously made him feel. Comparable to his sensation when he saw someone press an open book flat and complacently, irreparably crack the spine.

Bech's tuxedo over the years had developed a waxen sheen and grown small; throughout Goldy's party, his waist was being cruelly pinched. The taxicab, so capacious that Bech felt like ballast, turned down a succession of smaller and smaller streets and stopped on a dead-end loop, where, with the mystic menace of a Christmas tree, a portico blazed. The doorknocker was a goldsmith's hammer inscribed with a florid double "J." A servant in blue livery admitted Bech. Goldy bustled forward in a red velvet jacket and flopping ruffles. Another servant poured Bech a warm Scotch. Goldy, his eyes shuttling like a hockey player's, steered Bech past a towering pier glass into a room where beautiful women in cream and saffron and magenta drifted and billowed in soft slow motion. Men in black stood like channel markers in this sea. "Here's a lovely person you must meet," Goldy told Bech. To her he said, "Henry Bech. He's very shy. Don't frighten him away, darling."

She was an apparition—wide powdery shoulders, long untroubled chin ever so faintly cleft, lips ghostly in their cushioned perfection, gray eyes whose light flooded their cages of false lash and painted shadow. Bech asked her, "What do you do?"

She quivered; the corners of her lips trembled wryly, and he realized that the question had been

consummately stupid, that merely to rise each morning and fill her skin to the brim with such loveliness
was enough for any woman to do.

But she said, "Well, I have a husband, and five
children, and I've just published a book."

"A novel?" Bech could see it now: robin's-egg-blue
jacket, brisk adultery on country weekends, comic
relief provided by precocious children.

"No, not really. It's the history of labor movements
in England before 1860."

"Were there many?"

"Some. It was very difficult for them."

"How lovely of you," Bech said, "to care; that is,
when you look so"—he rejected "posh"—"unlabo-
rious."

Again, her face underwent, not a change of expression, which was unvaryingly sweet and atten-
tive, but a seismic tremor, as if her composure
restrained volcanic heat. She asked, "What are your
novels about?"

"Oh, ordinary people."

"Then how lovely of *you*; when you're so extraor-
dinary."

A man bored with being a channel marker came
and touched her elbow, and statelily she turned,
leaving Bech her emanations, like an astronomer
flooded by radio waves from a blank part of the sky.
He tried to take a fix on her flattery by looking, as
he went for another drink, into a mirror. His nose
with age had grown larger and its flanges had turned
distinctly red; his adaption of the hair style of the

young had educed woolly bursts of gray above his
ears and a tallowish mass of white curling outwards
at the back of his collar: he looked like a mob-
controlled congressman from Queens hoping to be
taken for a Southern senator. His face was pasty
with fatigue, though his eyes seemed frantically
alive. He observed in the mirror, observing him, a
slim young African woman in see-through pajamas.
He turned and asked her, "What *can* we do about
Biafra?"

"*Je le regrette, Monsieur,*" she said, "*mais main-
tenant je ne pense jamais. Je vis, simplement.*"

"*Parce que,*" Bech offered, "*le monde est trop
effrayant?*"

She shrugged. "*Peut-être.*" When she shrugged,
her silhouetted breasts shivered with their weight;
it took Bech back to his avid youthful perusals of
the *National Geographic*. He said, "*Je pense, comme
vous, que le monde est difficile à comprener, mais
certainement, en tout cas, vous êtes très sage, très
belle.*" But his French was not good enough to hold
her, and she turned, and was wearing bikini under-
pants, with tiger stripes, beneath the saffron gauze
of her pantaloons. Blue servants rang chimes for dinner. He gulped his drink, and avoided the sideways
eye of the congressman from Queens.

On his right was seated a middle-aged Lady of
evident importance, though her beauty could never
have been much more than a concentrate of sharp-
ness and sparkle. "You American Jews," she said, "are
so romantic. You think every little dolly bird is De-

lilah. I hate the 'pity me' in all your books. Women don't want to be complained at. They want to be screwed."

"I'll have to try it," Bech said.

"Do. Do." She pivoted toward a long-toothed gallant waiting grinning on her right; he exclaimed "Darling!" and their heads fell together like bagged oranges. On Bech's left sat a magenta shape his first glance had told him to ignore. It glittered and was young. Bech didn't trust anyone under thirty; the young now moved with the sacred and dangerous assurance of the old when he had been young. She was toying with her soup like a child. Her hand was small as a child's, with close-cut fingernails and endearing shadows around the knuckles. He felt he had seen the hand before. In a novel. *Lolita? Magic Mountain?* Simple etiquette directed that he ask her how she was.

"Rotten, thanks."

"Think of me," Bech said. "By the time I woke up in, it's four o'clock in the morning."

"I hate sleep. I don't sleep for days sometimes and feel wonderful. I think people sleep too much, that's why their arteries harden." In fact, he was to discover that she slept as the young do, in long easy swings that gather the extra hours into their arc and override all noise—though she had every woman's tendency to stir at dawn. She went on, as if politely, "Do you have hard arteries?"

"Not to my knowledge. Just impotence and gout."

"That sounds come-ony."

"Forgive me. I was just told women don't like being complained to."

"I heard the old tart say that. Don't believe her. They love it. Why are you impotent?"

"Old age?" A voice inside him said, *Old age? he tentatively said.*

"Come off it." He liked her voice, one of those British voices produced halfway down the throat, rather than obliquely off the sinuses, with alarming octave jumps. She was wearing gold granny glasses on her little heart-shaped face. He didn't know if her cheeks were flushed or rouged. He was pleased to observe that, though she was petite, her breasts pushed up plumply from her dress, which was orna- mented with small mirrors. Her lips, chalky and cush- ioned, with intelligent tremulous corners, seemed taken from the first woman he had met, as if one had been a preliminary study for the other. He noticed she had a little mustache, faint as two erased pencil lines. She told him, "You write."

"I used to."

"What happened?"

A gap in the dialogue. Fill in later. "I don't seem to know."

"I used to be a wife. My husband was an Ameri- can. Still is, come to think of it."

"Where did you live?" The girl and Bech simul- taneously glanced down and began to hurry to finish the food on their plates.

"New York."

"Like it?"

"Loved it."

"Didn't it seem dirty to you?"

"Gloriously." She chewed. He pictured sharp small even teeth lacerating and compressing bloody beef. He set down his fork. She swallowed and asked, "Love London?"

"Don't know it."

"You don't?"

"Been here only long enough to look at daffodils."

"I'll show it to you."

"How can you? How can I find you again?" Victorian novel? Rewrite.

"You're in London alone?"

A crusty piece of Yorkshire pudding looked too good to leave. Bech picked up his fork again, agreeing, "Mm. I'm alone everywhere."

"Would you like to come home with me?"

The lady on his right turned and said, "I must say, you're a stinker to let this old fag monopolize me."

"Don't complain. Men hate it."

She responded, "Your hair is smashing. You're almost Santa Claus."

"Tell me, love, who's this, what do you say, bird on my left?"

"She's Little Miss Poison. Her father bought himself a peerage from Macmillan."

The girl at Bech's back tickled the hairs of his neck with her breath and said, "I withdraw my invitation."

"Let's all," Bech said loudly, "have some more wine," pouring. The man with long teeth put his hand over the top of his glass. Bech expected a magician's trick but was disappointed.

And at the door, as Bech tried to sneak past the voracious pier glass with the girl, Goldy seemed disappointed. "But did you meet *every*body? These are the nicest people in London."

Bech hugged his publisher. Waxy old tux, meet velvet and ruffles. Learn how the other half lives. "Goldy," he said, "the party was nice, nicey, niciest. It couldn't have been nicier. Like, wow, out of sight." He saw drunken noise as the key to his exit. Otherwise this velvet gouger would milk him for another hour of lionization. Grr.

Goldy displayed the racial gracefulness in defeat. His limpid eyes, as busy as if he were playing blitz chess, flicked past Bech's shoulder to the girl. "Merissa dear, *do* take decent care of our celebrity. My fortune rides on his charm." Thus Bech learned her first name.

The taxi, with two in it, felt less like a hollow hull and more like a small drawing room, where voices needn't be raised. They did not, perhaps oddly, touch. *Perhaps oddly?* He had lost all ability to phrase. He was on the dark side of the earth in a cab with a creature whose dress held dozens of small mirrors. Her legs were white like knives, crossed and recrossed. A triangular bit of punctuation where the thighs ended. The cab moved through empty streets, past wrought-iron gates inked onto the sky and granite museums frowning beneath the weight of their entablatures, across the bright loud gulch of

Hyde Park Corner and Park Lane, into darker quieter streets. They passed a shuttered building that Merissa identified as the Chinese Communist Embassy. They entered a region where the shaggy heads of trees seemed to be dreaming of fantastically long colonnades and of high white wedding-cake façades receding to infinity. The cab stopped. Merissa paid. She let him in by a door whose knob, knocker, and mail slot were silken with polishings. Marble stairs. Another door. Another key. The odors of floor wax, of stale cigarette smoke, of narcissi in a pebbled bowl. Brandy with its scorched, expensive smell was placed beneath his nose. Obediently he drank. He was led into a bedroom. Perfume and powder, leather and an oil-clothy scent that took him back into English children's books that his mother, bent on his "improvement," used to buy at the Fifth Avenue Scribner's. A window opened. Chill April smells. *Winter kept us warm.* She brushed back curtains. A slice of slate night yellowish above the trees. The lights of an airplane winking in descent. A rustling all around him. The candy taste of lipstick. Clean air, warm skin. *Feeding a little life with dried tubers.* Her bare back a lunar surface beneath his hands. The forgotten impression of intrusion, of subtle monstrous assault, that the particularities of a new woman's body make upon us. *Summer surprised us.* Must find out her last name. There are rings of release beyond rings. Bech discovered in the bliss—the pang of relief around his waist—of taking off his tuxedo. Must see a tailor.

. . .

"When you were writing *The Chosen*," Tuttle asked, "did you deliberately set out to create a more flowery style?" This time he had brought a tape recorder. They were in Bech's hotel rooms, an extensive corner suite with a fake fireplace and a bed that hadn't been slept in. The fireplace was not entirely fake; it held a kind of crinkly plastic sculpture of a coal fire that glowed when plugged in and even gave off an imitation of heat.

"I never think about style, about creating one," Bech dictated into the baby microphone of the tape recorder. "My style is always as simple as the subject matter permits. As you grow older, though, you find that few things are simple."

"For example?"

"For example, changing a tire. I'm sorry, your question seems inane to me. This interview seems inane."

"Let me try another approach," Tuttle said, as maddeningly patient as a child psychiatrist. "In *Brother Pig*, were you conscious of inserting the political resonances?"

Bech blinked. "I'm sorry, when you say 'resonances' all I see is dried grapes. *Brother Pig* was about what its words said it was about. It was not a mask for something else. I do not write in code. I depend upon my reader for a knowledge of the English language and some acquired vocabulary of human experience. My books, I hope, would be unintelligible to baboons or squid. My books are human transactions—flirtations, quarrels."

"You're tired," Tuttle told him.

He was right. Merissa had taken him to a restaurant along Fulham Road run by fairies and then to Revolution, where big posters of Ho and Mao and Engels and Lenin watched from the walls as young people dressed in sequins and bell-bottoms jogged up and down within a dense, throbbing, coruscating fudge of noise. Bech knew something was happening here, a spiritual upthrusting like Christianity among the slaves of Rome or cabalism among the peasant Jews of stagnant Slavic Europe, but his old-fashioned particularizing vision kept dissolving the mob into its components: working girls resigned to a groggy tomorrow at their typewriters; neutered young men in fashion or photography to whom coming here was work; the truly idle, the rich and the black, escaping from the empty-eye-socket stare of spooked hours; the would-be young like himself, ancient lecherous woolly-haired Yanks whose willy-nilly charm and backwards success had prevented their learning ever to come in out of the rain; enigmatic tarty birds like Merissa, whose flat, he had discovered, held a room full of electric toys and teddy bears, with a bed where a child slept, her child, she confessed, a son, eight years old, born in America, when Merissa was nineteen, a child sent off to boarding school and even on vacations, Bech suspected, mostly taken to the park and the zoo by Isabella, Merissa's Spanish maid, an old round woman who peeked at Bech through doorways and then quickly, quietly shut the door . . . it was confusing. Revolution was the cave of a new religion but everyone had come, Bech saw, for reasons disappointingly reasonable and opportunistic. To make out. To be seen. To secure advancement. To be improved. That girl in the chain-link tunic and nothing else was working off her Yorkshire accent. That man flicking his arm like a dervish under the blue battering of the strobe lights was swinging a real-estate deal in his head. Bech doubted that the men on the wall approved what they saw. They were simple failed librarians like himself, schooled in the pre-Freudian verities. Hunger and pain are bad. Work is good. Men were made for the daylight. Orgasms are private affairs. *Down in Loo-siana/Where the alligators swim so mean* . . . Opposite him Merissa, who had a way of suddenly looking tall, though her smallness was what enchanted him, twinkled through the holes of her dress and moved her limbs and turned to him a shuddering profile, eyes shut as if better to feel the beat between her legs, that fluttering elusive beat: *What we are witnessing,* Bech announced inside his own head, in his role of college circuit-rider, *is the triumph of the clitoral, after three thousand years of phallic hegemony.* She called over to him, through the flashing din, "It gets to be rather same-y, doesn't it?" And he felt then his heart make the motion he had been waiting for, of love for her; like the jaws of a clam when the muscle is sliced, his heart opened. He tasted it, the sugary nip of impossibility. For he was best at loving what he could never have.

"Lord, you're lovely," he said. "Let's go home."

She accused him: "You don't love London, only me."

His conversations with Merissa did have a way of breaking into two-liners. For example,

MERISSA: "I'm terribly tired of being white."

BECH: "But you're so good at it."

Or:

BECH: "I've never understood what sex is like for a woman."

MERISSA (*thinking hard*): "It's like—fog."

The phone rang at nine the next morning. It was Tuttle. Goldschmidt had given him Merissa's number. Bech thought of expostulating but since the boy never drank he would have no idea how Bech's head felt. With some dim idea of appeasing those forces of daylight and righteous wrath that he had seen mocked on the walls of Revolution last night, he consented to meet Tuttle at his hotel at ten. Perhaps this stab at self-abnegation did him good, for, on his way to the West End in the lurching, swaying upstairs of a 74 bus, nauseated by the motion, having breakfasted on unbuttered toast and reheated tea (Merissa had observed his departure by sighing and rolling over onto her stomach, and her refrigerator held nothing but yogurt and champagne), gazing down upon the top of the shoppers in Baker Street— shimmering saris, polka-dot umbrellas—Bech was visited by inspiration. The title of his new novel abruptly came to him: Think Big. It balanced the title of his first, *Travel Light*. It held in the girders of its consonants, braced by those two stark "i"s, America's promise, pathos, crassness, grandeur. As *Travel Light* had been about a young man, so *Think Big* must be about a young woman, about openness and confusion, coruscation and the loss of the breeding function. Merissa could be the heroine. But she was British. Transposing her into an American would meet resistance at a hundred points, as for instance when she undressed, and was as white as an Artemis of marble, whereas any American girl that age carries all winter the comical ghost of last summer's bikini, emphasizing her erogenous zones like a diagram. And Merissa's enchanting smallness, the manner in which her perfection seemed carried out on an elfin scale, so that Bech could study by lamplight the bones of an ankle and foot as he would study an ivory miniature, a smallness excitingly violated when her mouth swam into the dimensions of the normal—this too was un-American. Your typical Bennington girl wore a 9½ sneaker and carried her sex as in a knapsack, to be unpacked at night. A rugged Boy/Girl Scout was the evolutionary direction, not the perfumed, faintly treacherous femininity Merissa exuded from each dear pore. Still, Bech reasoned while the bus maneuvered into Oxford Street and the shoppers danced in psychedelic foreshortening, she was not quite convincing as she was (what did she *do?* for instance, to warrant that expensive flat, and Isabella, and a dinner invitation from Goldy, and the closets full of swinging clothes, not to mention riding chaps and mud-crusted golf

shoes) and Bech was sure he could fill in her gaps
with bits of American women, could indeed re-create
her from almost nothing, needing less than a rib,
needing only a living germ of his infatuation, of his
love. Already small things from here and there, kept
alive by some kink in his forgetting mechanism, had
begun to fly together, to fit. A dance hall he had
once walked upstairs to, off of war-darkened Broadway. A rabid but deft Trotskyite barber his father
had patronized. The way New York's side streets
seek the sunset, and the way on Fifth Avenue hard-
shinned women in sunglasses hurry past languorous
mannequins in gilded robes, black-velvet cases of
jewels wired to burglar alarms, shopwindows crying
out ignored. But what would be the action of the
book (it was a big book, he saw, with a blue jacket
of coated stock and his unsmiling photo full on the
back, bled top and bottom), its conflict, its issue,
its outcome? The answer, like the title, came from
so deep within him that it seemed a message from
beyond: Suicide. His heroine must kill herself. Think
big. His heart trembled in excitement, at the enor-
mity of his crime.

"You're tired," Tuttle said, and went on, "I've seen
the point raised about your work, that the kind of
ethnic loyalty you display, loyalty to a narrow in-
dividualistic past, is divisive, and encourages war,
and helps account for your reluctance to join the
peace movement and the social revolution. How
would you rebut this?"

"Where did you see this point raised, did you say?"

"Some review."

"*What* review? Are you sure you just didn't make it up? I've seen some dumb things written about me, but never anything quite that vapid and doctrinaire."

"My attempt, Mr. Bech, is to elicit from you your opinions. If you find this an unfruitful area, let's move on. Maybe I should stop the machine while you collect your thoughts. We're wasting tape."

"Not to mention my lifeblood." But Bech groggily tried to satisfy the boy; he described his melancholy feelings in the go-go place last night, his intuition that self-aggrandizement and entrepreneurial energy were what made the world go and that slogans and movements to the contrary were evil dreams, evil in that they distracted people from particular, concrete realities, whence all goodness and effectiveness derive. He was an Aristotelian and not a Platonist. Write him down, if he must write him down as something, as a disbeliever; he disbelieved in the Pope, in the Kremlin, in the Vietcong, in the American eagle, in astrology, Arthur Schlesinger, Eldridge Cleaver, Senator Eastland, and Eastman Kodak. Nor did he believe overmuch in his disbelief. He thought intelligence a function of the individual and that groups of persons were intelligent in inverse proportion to their size. Nations had the brains of an amoeba whereas a committee approached the condition of a trainable moron. He believed, if this tape recorder must know, in the goodness of something vs. nothing, in the dignity of the inanimate, the intricacy of the animate, the beauty of the average woman, and the common sense of the average man. The tape spun out its reel and ran flapping.

Tuttle said, "That's great stuff, Mr. Bech. One more session, and we should have it."

"Never, never, never, never," Bech said. Something in his face drove Tuttle out the door. Bech fell asleep on his bed in his clothes. He awoke and found that *Think Big* had died. It had become a ghost of a book, an empty space beside the four faded spines that he had already brought to exist. *Think Big* had no content but wonder, which was a blankness. He thought back through his life, so many dreams and wakings, so many faces encountered and stoplights obeyed and streets crossed, and there was nothing solid; he had rushed through his life as through a badly chewed meal, leaving an ache of indigestion. In the beginning, the fresh flame of his spirit had burned everything clean—the entire gray city, stone and soot and stoops. Miles of cracked pavement had not been too much. He had gone to sleep on the sound of sirens and woken to the cries of fruit carts. There had been around him a sheltering ring of warm old tall bodies whose droning appeared to be wisdom, whose crooning and laughter seemed to be sifted down from the God who presided above the smoldering city's tip lights. There had been classrooms smelling of eraser crumbs, and strolling evenings when the lights of New Jersey seemed strung gems, and male pals from whom to learn loyalty and stoicism, and the first dizzying drag on a cigarette, and the first girl who let his hands linger, and the first joys of fabrication, of invention and completion.

Then unreality had swept in. It was his fault; he had wanted to be noticed, to be praised. He had wanted to be a man in the world, a "writer." For his punishment they had made from the sticks and mud of his words a coarse large doll to question and torment, which would not have mattered except that he was trapped inside the doll, shared a name and bank account with it. And the life that touched and brushed other people, that played across them like a saving breeze, could not break through the crust to him. He was, with all his brave talk to Tuttle of individual intelligence and the foolishness of groups, too alone.

He telephoned Goldschmidt, Ltd., and was told Goldy was out to lunch. He called Merissa but her number did not answer. He went downstairs and tried to talk to the hotel doorman about the weather. "Well, sir, weather is weather, I find to be the case generally. Some days is fine, and others a bit dim. This sky today you'll find is about what we generally have this time of the year. It'll all average out when we're in the grave, isn't that the truth of it, sir?" Bech disliked being humored, and the gravedigger scene had never been one of his favorites. He went walking beneath the dispirited, homogenous sky, featureless but for some downward wisps of nimbus promising rain that never arrived. Where were the famous English clouds, the clouds of Constable and Shelley? He tried to transplant the daffodils to Riverside Park, for his novel, but couldn't see them there, among those littered thickets hollowed by teen-aged layabouts bloodless with heroin, these British bulbs laid out in their loamy bed by ancient bowed men, the great-grandchildren of feudalism, who swept the paths where Bech walked with brooms, yes, and this was cheering, with brooms fashioned of twigs honestly bound together with twine. It began to rain.

Bech became a docile tourist and interviewee. He bantered on the B.B.C. Third Programme with a ripe-voiced young Welshman. He read from his works to bearded youths at the London School of Economics, between strikes. He submitted to a cocktail party at the U. S. Embassy. He participated in a television discussion on the Collapse of the American Dream with an edgy homosexual historian whose toupee kept slipping; a mug-shaped small man who thirty years ago had invented a donnish verse form resembling the limerick; a preposterously rude young radical with puffed-out lips and a dominating stammer; and, chairing their discussion, a tall B.B.C. girl whose elongated thighs kept arresting Bech in mid-sentence—she had pop eyes and a wild way of summing up, as if all the while she had been attending to angel-voices entirely her own. Bech let Merissa drive him, in her beige Fiat, to Stonehenge and Canterbury. At Canterbury she got into a fight with

a verger about exactly where Becket had been
stabbed. She took Bech to a concert in Albert Hall,
whose cavernous interior Bech drowsily confused
with Victoria's womb, and where he fell asleep.
Afterward they went to a club with gaming rooms
where Merissa, playing two blackjack hands simultaneously, lost sixty quid in twenty minutes. There
was a professional fierceness about the way she sat
at the green felt table that requickened his curiosity
as to what she *did*. He was sure she did something.
Her flat held a swept-off desk, and a bookcase
shelf solid with reference works. Bech would have
snooped, but he felt Isabella always watching him,
and the daylight hours he spent here were few. Merissa told him her last name—Merrill, the name of her
American husband—but fended off his other in-
quiries with the protest that he was being "writery"
and the disarming request that he consider her as
simply his "London episode." But how did she live?
She and her son and her maid. "Oh," Merissa told
him, "my father owns things. Don't ask me what
things. He keeps buying different ones."

He had not quite given up the idea of making
her the heroine of his masterpiece. He must understand what it is like to be young now. "The other
men you sleep with—what do you feel toward them?"

"They seem nice at the time."

"At the time; and then afterward not so nice?"

The suggestion startled her; from the way her eyes
widened, she felt he was trying to insert evil into
her world. "Oh yes, then too. They're so grateful.

Men are. They're so grateful if you just make them a cup of tea in the morning."

"But where is it all going? Do you think about marrying again?"

"Not much. That first go was pretty draggy. He kept saying things like, 'Pick up your underwear,' and, 'In Asia they live on ninety dollars a year.'" Merissa laughed.

Her hair was a miracle, spread out on the pillow in the morning light, a lustrous mass measured in infinity, every filament the same lucid black, a black that held red light within it as matter holds heat— whereas even of the hairs on his toes some had turned white. Gold names on an honor roll. As a character, Merissa would become a redhead, with that vulnerable freckled pallor and overlarge, uneven, earnest front teeth. Merissa's teeth were so perfectly spaced they seemed machined. Like her eyelashes. *Stars with a talent for squad-drill.* As she laughed, divulging the slippery grotto beyond her palate, Bech felt abhorrence rising in his throat. He looked toward the window; an airplane was descending from a ceiling of gray. He asked, "Do you take drugs?"

"Not really. A little grass to be companionable. I don't believe in it."

Her American counterpart would, of course. Bech saw this counterpart in his mind: a pale Puritan, self-destructive, her blue eyes faded like cotton work clothes too often scrubbed. Merissa's green eyes sparkled; her hectic cheeks burned. "What do you believe in?" he asked.

"Different things at different times," she said. "You don't seem all that pro-marriagey yourself."

"I am, for other people."

"I know why sleeping with you is so exciting. It's like sleeping with a parson."

"Dear Merissa," Bech said. He tried to crush her into himself. To suck the harlot's roses from her cheeks. He slobbered on her wrists, pressed his forehead against the small of her spine. He did all this in ten-point type, upon the warm white paper of her sliding skin. Poor child, under this old ogre, who had chewed his life so badly his stomach hurt, whose every experience was harassed by a fictional version of itself, whose waking life was a weary dream of echoes and erased pencil lines; he begged her forgiveness, while she moaned with anticipated pleasure. It was no use; he could not rise, he could not love her, could not perpetuate a romance or *roman* without seeing through it to the sour parting and the mixed reviews. He began, in lieu of performance, to explain this.

She interrupted: "Well, Henry, you must learn to replace ardor with art."

The cool practicality of this advice, its smug recourse to millennia of peasant saws and aristocratic maxims, to all that civilized wisdom America had sought to flee and find an alterantive to, angered him. "Art *is* ardor," he told her.

"Bad artists hope that's true."

"Read your Wordsworth."

"In tran*quill*ity, darling."

Her willingness to debate was beginning to excite him. He saw that wit and logic might survive into the lawless world coming to birth. "Merissa, you're so clever."

"The weak must be. That's what England is learning."

"Do you think I'm necessarily impotent? As an artist?"

"Unnecessarily."

"Merissa, tell me: what do you *do?*"

"You'll see," she said, pressing her head back into the pillow and smiling in assured satisfaction, as his giant prick worked back and forth. The tail wagging the dog.

Tuttle caught him at his hotel the day before he left and asked him if he felt any affinity with Ronald Firbank. "Only the affinity," Bech said, "I feel with all Roman Catholic homosexuals."

"I was hoping you'd say something like that. How are you feeling, Mr. Bech? The last time I saw you, you looked awful. Frankly."

"I feel better now that you've stopped seeing me."

"Great. It was a real privilege and delight for me, I tell you. I hope you like the way the piece shaped up; I do. I hope you don't mind my few reservations."

"No, you can't go anywhere these days without reservations."

"Ha ha." It was the only time Bech ever heard Tuttle laugh.

Merissa didn't answer her telephone. Bech hoped she'd be at the farewell party Goldy threw for him—a modest affair, without blue servants, and Bech in his altered tuxedo the sole man present in formal dress—but she wasn't. When Bech asked where she was, Goldy said tersely, "Working. She sends her love and regrets." Bech called her at midnight, at one in the morning, at two, at five when the birds began singing, at seven when the earliest church bells rang, at nine and at ten, while packing to catch his plane. Not even Isabella answered. She must be off on a country weekend. Or visiting the boy at school. Or vanished like a good paragraph in a book too bulky to reread.

Goldschmidt drove him to the airport in his maroon Bentley, and with an urgent prideful air pressed a number of Sunday newspapers upon him. "The *Observer* gave us more space," he said, "but the *Times* seemed to like it more. All in all, a very fine reception for a, let's be frank, a rather trumped-up mishmash of a book. Now you must do us a blockbuster." He said this, but his eyes were darting over Bech's shoulder toward the stream of fresh arrivals.

"I have just the title," Bech told him. He saw he must put Goldy into it, as a Jewish uncle. A leather-worker, his right palm hard as a turtle shell from handling an awl. That heavy pampered Florentine head bent full of greedy dreams beneath a naked light bulb, as pocketbooks, belts, and sandals tumbled from the slaughter of screaming calves. The baroque beauty of the scraps piled neglected at his feet. A fire escape out the window. Some of the panes were transparent wire-glass and others, unaccountably, were painted opaque.

Goldschmidt added a folded tabloid to Bech's supply of airplane reading.

PEER, BRIDE NABBED
IN DORSET DOPE RAID

the headline said. Goldschmidt said, "Page seventeen might amuse you. As you know, this is the paper Merissa's father bought last year. Millions read it."

"No, I didn't know. She told me nothing about her father."

"He's a dear old rascal. Almost the last of the true Tories."

"I could have sworn she was a Lib-Lab."

"Merissa is a very clever lamb," Goldschmidt stated, and pinched his lips shut. In our long Diaspora we have learned not to tattle on our hosts. Goldy's right hand, shaken farewell, was unreally soft.

Bech saved page seventeen for the last. The *Times* review was headlined "More Ethnic Fiction from the New World" and lumped *The Best of Bech* with a novel about Canadian Indians by Leonard Cohen and a collection of protest essays and scatalogical poems by LeRoi Jones. The long *Observer* piece was titled "Bech's Best Not Good Enough" and was signed L. Clark Tuttle. Bech skimmed, as a fakir walks on hot coals, pausing nowhere long enough to

burn the moisture from the soles of his feet. Almost
none of the quotes he had poured into the boy's notebook and tape recorder were used. Instead, an ag-
grieved survey of Bech's *œuvre* unfolded, smudged
by feeble rebuttals.

. . . Queried concerning the flowery, not to say fruity, style
of *The Chosen,* Bech shrugged off the entire problem of style,
claiming (facetiously?) that he never thinks about it. . . .
Of the book's profound failure, the crippling irreconcilability
of its grandiose intentions and the triviality of its characters'
moral concerns, Bech appears blissfully unaware, taking
refuge in the charming, if rather automatically gnomic, dis-
claimer that "as you grow older, life becomes complicated"
. . . This interviewer was struck, indeed, by the defensive
nature of Bech's breezy garrulousness; his charm operates as
a screen against others—their menacing opinions, the raw
stuff of their life—just as, perhaps, drink operates within him
as a screen against his own deepest self-suspicions . . .
counter-revolutionary nostalgia . . . possibly ironical faith in
"entrepreneurism" . . . nevertheless, undoubted verbal gifts
. . . traumatized by the economic collapse of the 1930's . . .
a minor master for the space of scattered pages . . . not to
be classed, Bech's faithful *New York Review* claque to the
contrary, with the early Bellow or the late Mailer . . . reminded, in the end, after the butterfly similes and overex-
tended, substanceless themes of this self-anointed "Best," of
(and the comparison may serve English readers as an index
of present relevance) Ronald Firbank!

Bech let the paper go limp. The airplane had
taxied out and he braced himself for the perilous
plunge into flight. Only when aloft, with Hampton
Court securely beneath him, a delicate sepia diagram
of itself, and London's great stone mass dissolved
into a cloud behind him, did Bech turn to page seven-

teen. A column there was headed MERISSA'S WEEK. The line drawing of the girl reminded Bech erotically of the spaces in her face—the catlike span between her eyes, the painted circles of her cheeks, the sudden moist gap of her mouth, which in the caricature existed as a wry tilde, a ~.

Merissa had a tamey week * * * The daffodils were just like olde tymes, eh, W. W.? * * * Beware: the blackjack dealer at L'Ambassadeur draws to fifteen and always makes it * * * A verger down at Canterbury C. is such an ignoramus I took him for a Drugs Squad agent * * * The new acoustics in Albert Hall are still worse than those on Salisbury Plain* * * John & Oko will cut their next record standing on their heads, their bottoms painted to resemble each other * * * Swinging L. was a shade more swingy this week when the darling American author Henry (*Travel Light, Brother Pig* and don't look blank they're in Penguins) Bech dropped in at Revolution and other In spots. The heart of many a jaded bird beat brighter to see Bech's rabbinical curls bouncing in time to "Poke Salad Annie" and other Now hits. Merissa says: Hurry Back, H. B., transatlantic men are the most existential * * * He was visiting Londinium to help push la crème of his crème, *Bech's Best,* a J. J. Goldschmidt release, with a dull, dull jacket—the author's pic is missing. Confidentially, his heart belongs to dirty old New York * * *

Bech closed his eyes, feeling his love for her expand as the distance between them increased. Entrepreneurism rides again. *Rabbinical curls:* somehow he had sold her that. *Automatically gnomic:* he had sold that too. *As a screen against others.* Firbank dead at forty. Still gaining altitude, he realized he was not dead; his fate was not so substantial. He had become a character by Henry Bech.

Bech Enters Heaven

WHEN HENRY BECH was an impressionable pre-adolescent of thirteen, more bored than he would admit with the question of whether or not the 1936 Yankees could wrest the pennant back from Detroit, his mother one May afternoon took him out of school, after consultation with the principal; she was a hard-ened consulter with the principal. She had consulted when Henry entered the first grade, when he came back from the second with a bloody nose, when he skipped the third, when he was given a 65 in Penman-ship in the fifth, and when he skipped the sixth. The school was P.S. 87, at Seventy-seventh and Amster-dam—a bleak brick building whose interior complex-ity of smells and excitement, especially during a snowstorm or around Hallowe'en, was transcendent. None but very young hearts could have withstood the daily strain of so much intrigue, humor, desire, personality, mental effort, emotional current, of so many achingly important nuances of prestige and impersonation. Bech, rather short for his age, yet with a big nose and big feet that promised future growth, was recognized from the first by his classmates as an only son, a mother's son more than a father's, pampered and bright though not a prodigy (his voice had no pitch, his mathematical aptitude was no Einstein's); naturally he was teased. Not all the teasing took the form of bloody noses; sometimes the girl in the adjacent desk-seat tickled the hair on his forearms with her pencil, or his name was flaunted through the wire fence that separated the sexes at recess. The brownstone neighborhoods that supplied students to the school were in those years still middle-class, if by middle-class is understood not a level of poverty (unlike today's poor, they had no cars, no credit and delivery arrangements with the liquor store) but of self-esteem. Immersed in the Great Depression, they had kept their families together, kept their feet from touching bottom, and kept their faith in the future—their children's future more than their own. These children brought a giddy relief into the sanctum of the school building, relief that the world, or at least this brick cube carved from it, had survived another day. How fragile the world felt to them!—as fragile as it seems sturdy to today's children, who wish to destroy it. Predominately Jewish, Bech's grammar school classes had a bold bright dash of German Gentiles, whose fathers also kept a small shop or plied a manual craft, and some Eastern Europeans, whose fey manners and lisped English made them the centers of romantic frenzy and wild joking attacks. At this time Negroes, like Chinese, were exotic oddities, created, like zebras, in jest. All studied, by the light of yellowish overhead globes and of the 48-star flag nailed above the blackboard, penmanship, the spice routes, the imports and exports of the three Guianas, the three cases of percentage, and other matters of rote given significance by the existence of breadlines and penthouses, just as the various drudgeries of their fathers were given dignity, even holiness, by their direct connection with food and survival. Although he would have been slow to admit this also, little Bech loved the school; he cherished his citizenship in its ragged population, was enraptured by the freckled chin and cerulean eyes of Eva Hassel across the aisle, and detested his mother's frequent interference in his American education. Whenever she appeared outside the office of the principal (Mr. Linnehan, a sore-lidded spoiled priest with an easily mimicked blink and stammer), he was teased in the cloakroom or down on the asphalt at recess; whenever she had him skipped a grade, he became all the more the baby of the class. By the age of thirteen, he was going to school with girls that were women. That day in May, he showed his anger with his mother by not talking to her as they walked from the scarred school steps, down Seventy-eighth, past a mock-Tudor apartment house like some evilly enlarged and begrimed fairy-tale chalet, to Broadway and Seventy-ninth and the

IRT kiosk with its compounded aroma of hot brakes, warm bagels, and vomit.

Extraordinarily, they took a train *north*. The whole drift of their lives was *south*—south to Times Square and to the Public Library, south to Gimbels, south to Brooklyn where his father's two brothers lived. North, there was nothing but Grant's Tomb, and Harlem, and Yankee Stadium, and Riverdale where a rich cousin, a theatre manager, inhabited an apartment full of glass furniture and an array of leering and scribbled photographs. North of that yawned the foreign vastness, first named New York State but melting westward into other names, other states, where the *goyim* farmed their farms and drove their roadsters and swung on their porch swings and engaged in the countless struggles of moral heroism depicted continuously in the Hollywood movies at the Broadway RKO. Upon the huge body of the United States, swept by dust storms and storms of Christian conscience, young Henry knew that his island of Manhattan existed like a wart; relatively, his little family world was an immigrant enclave, the religion his family practiced was a tolerated affront, and the language of this religion's celebration was a backwards-running archaism. He and his kin and their kindred were huddled in shawls within an overheated back room while outdoors a huge and beautiful wilderness rattled their sashes with wind and painted the panes with frost; and all the furniture they had brought with them from Europe, the footstools and phylacteries, the copies of Tolstoy and Heine, the ambitiousness and defensiveness and love, belonged to this stuffy back room.

Now his mother was pointing him north, into the cold. Their reflections shuddered in the black glass as the express train slammed through local stops, wan islands of light where fat colored women waited with string shopping bags. Bech was always surprised that these frozen vistas did not shatter as they pierced them; perhaps it was the multi-leveled sliding, the hurtling metal precariously switched aside from collision, more than the odors and subterranean claustrophobia, that made the boy sick on subways. He figured that he was good for eight stops before nausea began. It had just begun when she touched his arm. High, high on the West Side they emerged, into a region where cliffs and windy hilltops seemed insecurely suppressed by the asphalt grid. A boisterous shout of spring rolled upward from the river, and unexpected bridges of green metal arched seraphically overhead. Together they walked, the boy and his mother, he in a wool knicker suit that scratched and sang between his legs, she in a tremulous hat of shining black straw, up a broad pavement bordered with cobblestones and trees whose bark was scabbed brown and white like a giraffe's neck. This was the last year when she was taller than he; his sideways glance reaped a child's cowing impression of, beneath the unsteady flesh of her jaw, the rose splotches at the side of her neck that signaled excitement or anger. He had better talk. "Where are we going?"

"So," she said, "the cat found his tongue."

"You know I don't like your coming into the school."

"Mister Touch-Me-Not," she said, "so ashamed of his mother he wants all his blue-eyed *shikses* to think he came out from under a rock, I suppose. Or better yet lives in a tree like Siegfried."

Somewhere in the past she had wormed out of him his admiration of the German girls at school. He blushed. "Thanks to you," he told her, "they're all two years older than me."

"Not in their empty golden heads, they're not so old. Maybe in their pants, but that'll come to you soon enough. Don't hurry the years, soon enough they'll hurry you."

Homily, flattery, and humiliation: these were what his mother applied to him, day after day, like a sculptor's pats. It deepened his blush to hear her mention Eva Hassel's pants. Were they what would come to him soon enough? This was her style, to mock his reality and stretch his expectations. "Mother, don't be fantastic."

"Ai, nothing fantastic. There's nothing one of those golden girls would like better than fasten herself to some smart little Jewish boy. Better that than some sausage-grinding Fritz who'll go to beer and beating her before he's twenty-five. You keep your nose in your books."

"That's where it was. Where are you taking me?"

"To see something more important than where to put your *putz*."

"Mother, don't be vulgar."

"Vulgar is what I call a boy who wants to put his

mother under a rock. His mother and his people and his brain, all under a rock."

"Now I understand. You're taking me to look at Plymouth Rock."

"Something like it. If you have to grow up American, at least let's not look only at the underside. Arnie"—the Riverdale cousin—"got me two tickets from Josh Glazer, to I don't know quite what it is. We shall see."

The hill beneath their feet flattened; they arrived at a massive building of somehow unsullied granite, with a paradoxical look of having been here forever yet having been rarely used. Around its top ran a ribbon of carved names: PLATO · NEWTON · AESCHYLUS · LEONARDO · AQUINAS · SHAKESPEARE · VOLTAIRE · COPERNICUS · ARISTOTLE · HOBBES · VICO · PUSHKIN · LINNAEUS · RACINE and infinitely on, around cornices and down the receding length of the building's two tall wings. Courtyard followed courtyard, each at a slightly higher level than the last. Conical evergreens stood silent guard; an unseen fountain played. For entrance, there was a bewildering choice of bronze doors. Bech's mother pushed one and encountered a green-uniformed guard; she told him. "My name is Hannah Bech and this is my son Henry. These are our tickets, it says right here this is the day, they were obtained for us by a close associate of Josh Glazer's, the playwright. Nobody forewarned me it would be such a climb from the subway, that's why I'm out of breath like this." The guard, and then another guard, for they several times got lost, directed them (his

mother receiving and repeating a full set of directions
each time) up a ramifying series of marble stairways
into the balcony of an auditorium whose ceiling, the
child's impression was, was decorated with plaster
toys—scrolls, masks, seashells, tops, and stars.

A ceremony was already in progress. Their dis-
cussions with the guards had consumed time. The
bright stage far below them supported a magical
tableau. On a curved dais composed of six or seven
rows a hundred persons, mostly men, were seated.
Though some of the men could be seen to move—one
turned his head, another scratched his knee—their
appearance in sum had an iron unity; they looked
engraved. Each face, even at the distance of the balcony, displayed the stamp of extra precision that de-
vout attention and frequent photography etch upon
a visage; each had suffered the crystallization of fame.
Young Henry saw that there were other types of
Heaven, less agitated and more elevated than the
school, more compact and less tragic than Yankee
Stadium, where the scattered players, fragile in white,
seemed about to be devoured by the dragon-shaped
crowd. He knew, even before his mother, with the
aid of a diagram provided on her program, began to
name names, that under his eyes was assembled the
flower of the arts in America, its rabbis and chieftains,
souls who while still breathing enjoyed their immortality.

The surface of their collective glory undulated as
one or another would stand, shuffle outward from his
row, seize the glowing lectern, and speak. Some rose

to award prizes; others rose to accept them. They applauded one another with a polite rustle eagerly echoed and thunderously amplified by the anonymous, perishable crowd on the other side of the veil, a docile cloudy multitude stretching backwards from front rows of corsaged loved ones into the dim regions of the balcony where mere spectators sat, where little Bech stared dazzled while his mother busily bent above the identifying diagram. She located, and pointed out to him, with that ardor for navigational detail that had delayed their arrival here, Emil Nordquist, the Bard of the Prairie, the beetle-browed celebrant in irresistible *vers libre* of shocked corn and Swedish dairymaids; John Kingsgrant Forbes, New England's dapper novelist of manners; Hannah Ann Collins, the wispy, mystical poet of impacted passion from Alabama, the most piquant voice in American verse since the passing of the Amherst recluse; the massive Jason Honeygale, Tennessee's fabled word-torrent; hawk-eyed Torquemada Langguth, lover and singer of California's sheer cliffs and sere unpopulated places; and Manhattan's own Josh Glazer, Broadway wit, comedywright, lyricist, and Romeo. And there were squat bald sculptors with great curved thumbs; red-bearded painters like bespattered prophets; petite, gleaming philosophers who piped Greek catchwords into the microphone; stooped and drawling historians from the border states; avowed Communists with faces as dry as paper and black ribbons dangling from their *pinces-nez;* atonal composers delicately exchanging awards and

reminiscences of Paris, the phrases in French nasally
cutting across their speech like accented trombones;
sibylline old women with bronze faces—all of them
unified, in the eyes of the boy Bech, by not only the
clothy dark mass of their clothes and the brilliance of
the stage but by their transcendence of time: they
had attained the haven of lasting accomplishment
and exempted themselves from the nagging nuisance of growth and its twin (which he precociously
felt in himself even then, especially in his teeth),
decay. He childishly assumed that, though unveiled
every May, they sat like this eternally, in the same
iron arrangement, beneath this domed ceiling of
scrolls and stars.

At last the final congratulation was offered, and the
final modest acceptance enunciated. Bech and his
mother turned to re-navigate the maze of staircases.
They were both shy of speaking, but she sensed, in
the abstracted way he clung to her side, neither welcoming nor cringing from her touch when she reached
to reassure him in the crowd, that his attention had
been successfully turned. His ears were red, showing
that an inner flame had been lit. She set him on a
track, a track that must be—Mrs. Bech ignored a sudden qualm, like a rude jostling from behind—the
right one.

Bech never dared hope to join that pantheon.
Those faces of the thirties, like the books he began to
read, putting aside baseball statistics forever, formed
a world impossibly high and apart, an immutable text

graven on the stone brow—his confused impression
was—of Manhattan. In middle age, it would startle
him to realize that Louis Bromfield, say, was no
longer considered a sage, that van Vechten, Cabell,
and John Erskine had become as obscure as the famous gangsters of the same period, and that an entire generation had grown to wisdom without once
chuckling over a verse by Arthur Guiterman or
Franklin P. Adams. When Bech received, in an envelope not so unlike those containing solicitations to
join the Erotica Book Club or the Associated Friends
of Apache Education, notice of his election to a society whose title suggested that of a merged church,
with an invitation to its May ceremonial, he did not
connect the honor with his truant afternoon of over
three decades ago. He accepted, because in his fal-
low middle years he hesitated to decline any invitation, whether it was to travel to Communist Europe
or to smoke marijuana. His working day was brief,
his living day was long, and there always lurked the
hope that around the corner of some impromptu ac-
quiescence he would encounter, in a flurry of apolo-
gies and excitedly mis-aimed kisses, his long-lost
mistress, Inspiration. He took a taxi north on the ap-
pointed day. By chance he was let off at a side entrance in no way reminiscent of the august frontal
approach he had once ventured within the shadow
of his mother. Inside the bronze door, Bech was
greeted by a mini-skirted secretary who, licking her
lips and perhaps unintentionally bringing her pelvis
to within an inch of his, pinned his name in plastic to
his lapel and, as a tantalizing afterthought, the tip of

her tongue exposed in playful concentration, adjusted the knot of his necktie. Other such considerate houris were supervising arrivals, separating antique *belle-lettrists* from their overcoats with philatelic care, steering querulously nodding poetesses toward the elevator, administering the distribution of gaudy heaps of name tags, admission cards, and coded numerals. His girl wore a button that said GOD FREAKS OUT.

Bech asked her, "Am I supposed to do anything?"

She said, "When your name is announced, stand."

"Do I take the elevator?"

She patted his shoulders and tugged one of his earlobes. "I think you're a young enough body," she judged, "to use the stairs."

He obediently ascended a thronged marble stairway and found himself amid a cloud of murmuring presences; a few of the faces were familiar—Tory Ingersoll, a tireless old fag, his prim features rigid in their carapace of orangish foundation, who had in recent years plugged himself into hipsterism and become a copious puffist and anthologist for the "new" poetry, whether concrete, non-associative, neo-gita, or plain protest; Irving Stern, a swarthy, ruminative critic of Bech's age and background, who for all his strenuous protests of McLuhanite openness had never stopped squinting through the dour goggles of Leninist aesthetics, and whose own prose style tasted like aspirin tablets being chewed; Mildred Beloussovsky-Dommergues, her name as polyglot as her marriages, her weight-lifter's shoulders and generous slash of a wise whore's mouth perversely dwindled in print to a trickle of elliptic dimeters; Char Ecktin, the revolutionary young dramatist whose foolish smile and high-pitched chortle consorted oddly with the facile bitterness of his dénouements—but many more were half-familiar, faces dimly known, like those of bit actors in B movies, or like those faces which emerge from obscurity to cap a surprisingly enthusiastic obituary, or those names which figure small on title pages, as translator, co-editor, or "as told to," faces whose air of recognizability might have been a matter of ghostly family resemblance, or of a cocktail party ten years ago, or a P.E.N. meeting, or of a moment in a bookstore, an inside flap hastily examined and then resealed into the tight bright row of the unpurchased. In this throng Bech heard his name softly called, and felt his sleeve lightly plucked. But he did not lift his eyes for fear of shattering the spell, of disturbing the penumbral decorum and rustle around him. They came to the end of their labyrinthine climb, and were ushered down a dubiously narrow corridor. Bech hesitated, as even the dullest steer hesitates in the slaughterer's chute, but the pressure behind moved him on, outward, into a spotlit tangle of groping men and scraping chairs. He was on a stage. Chairs were arranged in curved tiers. Mildred Belloussovsky-Dommergues waved an alabaster, muscular arm: "Yoo-hoo, Henry, over here. Come be a B with me." She even spoke now— so thoroughly does art corrupt the artist—in dimeters.

Willingly he made his way upwards toward her. Always, in his life, no matter how underfurnished in other respects, there had been a woman to shelter beside. The chair beside her bore his name. On the seat of the chair was a folded program. On the back of the program was a diagram. The diagram fitted a memory, and looking outward, into the populated darkness that reached backwards into a balcony, beneath a ceiling dimly decorated with toylike protrusions of plaster, Bech suspected, at last, where he was. With the instincts of a literary man he turned to printed matter for confirmation; he bent over the diagram and, yes, found his name, his number, his chair. He was here. He had joined that luminous, immutable tableau. He had crossed to the other side.

Now that forgotten expedition with his mother returned to him, and their climb through those ramifications of marble, a climb that mirrored, but profanely, the one he had just taken within sacred precincts; and he deduced that this building was vast twice over, an arch-like interior meeting in this domed auditorium where the mortal and the immortal could behold one another, through a veil that blurred and darkened the one and gave to the other a supernatural visibility, the glow and precision of Platonic forms. He studied his left hand—his partner in numerous humble crimes, his delegate in many furtive investigations—and saw it partaking, behind the flame-blue radiance of his cuff, joint by joint, to the quicks of his fingernails, in the fine articulation found less in reality than in the Promethean anatomical studies of Leonardo and Raphael.

Bech looked around; the stage was filling. He seemed to see, down front, where the stage light was most intense, the oft-photographed (by Steichen, by Karsh, by Cartier-Bresson) profile and vivid corn-silk hair of—it couldn't be—Emil Nordquist. The Bard of the Prairie still lived! He must be a hundred. No, well, if in the mid-thirties he was in his mid-forties, he would be only eighty now. While Bech, that pre-adolescent, was approaching fifty: time had treated him far more cruelly.

And now, through the other wing of the stage, from the elevator side, moving with the agonized shuffle-step of a semi-paralytic but still sartorially formidable in double-breasted chalkstripes and a high starched collar, entered John Kingsgrant Forbes, whose last perceptive and urbane examination of Beacon Hill mores had appeared in World War II, during the paper shortage. Had Bech merely imagined his obituary?

"Arriveth our queen," Mildred Belloussovsky-Dommergues sardonically murmured on his left, with that ambiguous trace of a foreign accent, the silted residue of her several husbands. And to Bech's astonishment in came, supported on the courtly arm of Jason Honeygale, whose epic bulk had shriveled to folds of veined hide draped over stegosaurian bones, the tiny tottering figure of Hannah Ann Collins, wearing the startled facial expression of the blind. She was led down front, where the gaunt figure of Torquemada Langguth, his spine bent nearly double, his falconine crest now white as an egret's, rose to greet her and feebly to adjust her chair.

Bech murmured leftwards, "I thought they were all dead."

Mildred airily answered, "We find it easier, not to die."

A shadow plumped brusquely down in the chair on Bech's right; it was—O, monstrous!—Josh Glazer. His proximity seemed to be a patron's, for he told Bech windily, "Jesus Christ, Bech, I've been plugging you for years up here, but the bastards always said, 'Let's wait until he writes another book, that last one was such a flop.' Finally I say to them, 'Look. The son of a bitch, he's *never* going to write another book,' so they say, 'O.K., let's let him the hell in.' Welcome aboard, Bech. Christ I've been a raving fan of yours since the Year One. When're you gonna try a comedy, Broadway's dead on its feet." He was deaf, his hair was dyed black, and his teeth were false too, for his blasts of breath carried with them a fetid smell of trapped alcohol and of a terrible organic something that suggested to Bech —touching a peculiar fastidiousness that was all that remained of his ancestors' orthodoxy—the stench of decayed shellfish. Bech looked away and saw everywhere on this stage dissolution and riot. The furrowed skulls of philosophers lolled in a Bacchic stupor. Wicked smirks flickered back and forth among faces enshrined in textbooks. Eustace Chubb, America's poetic conscience throughout the Cold

War, had holes in his socks and mechanically chafed a purple sore on his shin. Anatole Husač, the Father of Neo-Figurism, was sweating out a drug high, his hands twitching like suffocating fish. As the ceremony proceeded, not a classroom of trade-school dropouts could have been more impudently inattentive. Mildred Belloussovsky-Dommergues persistently tickled the hairs on Bech's wrist with the edge of her program; Josh Glazer offered him a sip from a silver flask signed by the Gershwin brothers. The leonine head—that of a great lexicographer—directly in front of Bech drifted sideways and emitted illegible snores. The Medal for Modern Fiction was being awarded to Kingsgrant Forbes; the cello-shaped critic (best known for his scrupulous editorship of the six volumes of Hamlin Garland's correspondence) began his speech, "In these sorry days of so-called Black Humor, of the fictional apotheosis of the underdeveloped," and a Negro in the middle of Bech's row stood, spoke a single black expletive, and, with much scraping of chairs, made his way from the stage. A series of grants was bestowed. One of the recipients, a tiptoeing fellow in a mauve jump suit, hurled paper streamers toward the audience and bared his chest to reveal painted there a psychedelic pig labeled Milhaus; at this, several old men, an Arizona naturalist and a New Deal muralist, stamped off, and for a long time could be heard buzzing for the elevator. The sardonic hubbub waxed louder. Impatience set in. "Goddammit," Josh Glazer breathed to Bech, "I'm paying a limou-

sine by the hour downstairs. Jesus and I've got a
helluva cute little fox waiting for me at the Plaza."

At last the time came to introduce the new members. The citations were read by a farsighted landscape painter who had trouble bringing his papers,
the lectern light, and his reading glasses into mutual
adjustment at such short focus. "Henry Bech," he
read, pronouncing it "Betch," and Bech confusedly
stood. The spotlights dazzled him; he had the sensation of being microscopically examined, and of being
strangely small. When he stood, he had expected
to rear into a man's height, and instead rose no taller
than a child.

"A native New Yorker," the citation began, "who
has chosen to sing of the continental distances—"

Bech wondered why writers in official positions
were always supposed to "sing"; he couldn't remember the last time he had even hummed.

"—a son of Israel loyal to Melville's romanticism—"

He went around telling interviewers Melville was
his favorite author, but he hadn't gotten a third of
the way through *Pierre*.

"—a poet in prose whose polish precludes pre- —
pro- —pardon me, these are new biofocals—"

Laughter from the audience. Who was out there
in that audience?

"—let me try again: whose polish precludes
prolifigacy—"

His mother was out there in that audience!

"—a magician of metaphor—"

She was there, right down front, basking in the

reflected stagelight, an orchid corsage pinned to her
bosom.

"—and a friend of the human heart."

But she had died four years ago, in a nursing home
in Riverdale. As the applause washed in, Bech saw
that the old lady with the corsage was applauding
only politely, she was not his mother but somebody
else's, maybe of the boy with the pig on his stomach,
though for a moment, a trick of the light, something
determined and expectant in the tilt of her head,
something hopeful . . . The light in his eyes turned
to warm water. His applause ebbed away. He sat
down. Mildred nudged him. Josh Glazer shook his
hand, too violently. Bech tried to clear his vision by
contemplating the backs of the heads. They were
blank: blank shabby backs of a cardboard tableau
lent substance only by the credulous, by old women
and children. His knees trembled, as if after an ardu-
ous climb. He had made it, he was here, in Heaven.
Now what?

APPENDIX A

We are grateful for permission to reprint corroborating excerpts from the unpublished Russian journal of Henry Bech. The journal, physically, is a faded red Expenses diary, measuring 7⅜" by 4¼", stained by Moscow brandy and warped by Caucasian dew. The entries, of which the latter are kept in red ballpoint pen, run from October 20, 1964, to December 6, 1964. The earliest are the fullest.

I

Oct. 20. Flight from NY at midnight, no sleep, Pan Am kept feeding me. Beating against the sun, soon dawn. Paris strange passing through by bus, tattered tired sepia sets of second-rate opera being wheeled through, false cheer of café awnings, waiting for chorus of lamplighters. Orly to Le Bourget. Moscow plane a new world. Men in dark coats waiting bunched. Solemn as gangsters. Overhead first understood Russian word, *Americanski*, pronounced with wink toward me by snaggle-toothed gent putting bulky black coat in overhead rack. Rack netted cord, inside ribs of plane show, no capitalist plastic. Stewardesses not our smoothly extruded tarts but hefty flesh; served us real potatoes, beef sausage, borsch. Aeroflot a feast afloat. Crowded happy stable smell, animal heat in cold stable, five miles up. Uncles' back rooms in Wmsburg. Babble around me, foreign languages strangely soothing, at home in Babel. Fell asleep on bosom of void, grateful to be alive, home. Woke in dark again. Earth's revolution full in my face. Moscow dim on ocean of blackness, delicate torn veil, shy of electricity, not New York, that rude splash. Premonition: no one will meet. Author Disappears Behind Iron Curtain. Bech Best Remembered for Early Work. A delegation with roses waiting for me on other side of glass pen, wait for hours, on verge of Russia, decompressing, time different here, steppes of time, long dully lit terminal, empty of ads. Limousine driven by voiceless back of head, sleigh driver in Tolstoy, long haul to Moscow, a wealth of darkness, gray birches, slim, young, far from gnarled American woods. In hotel spelled out этáж waiting for elevator, French hidden beneath the Cyrillic. Everywhere, secrets.

II

Oct. 23. Met Sobaka, head of Writers' U. Building Tolstoy's old manse, dining room baronial oak. Litterateurs live like aristocrats. Sobaka has lipless mouth, wild bark, must have strangled men with bare hands. Tells me long story of love of his poetry expressed by coalminers in the Urals. Skip translating: ". . . then, here in . . . the deepest part of the mine . . . by only the light of, uh, carbon lights in the miners' caps . . . for three hours I recited . . . from the works of my youth, lyrics of the fields and forests of Byelorussia. Never have I known such enthusiasm. Never have I possessed such inspiration, such, ah, powers of memory. At the end . . . they wept to see me depart . . . these simple miners . . . their coal-blackened faces streaked, ah, veined with the silver of tears."

"Fantastic," I say.

"*Fantastichni*," Skip translates.

Sobaka makes Skip ask me if I like the image, their faces of coal veined with silver.

"It's good," say I.

"*Korosho*," says Skip.

"The earth weeps precious metal," I say. "The world's working people weep at the tyranny of capital."

Skip guffaws but translates, and Sobaka reaches under table and seizes my thigh in murderous pinch of conspiracy.

Nov. 12. Back in Moscow, lunch at W.U. Sobaka in fine form, must have chopped off somebody's index finger this morning. Says trip to Irkutsk hazardous, airport might get snowed in. Hee hee hee. Suggests Kasakhstan instead, I say why not?—*nichyvo*. Eye-

ball to eyeball. He toasts Jack London, I toast Pushkin. He does Hemingway, I do Turgenev. I do
Nabokov, he counters with John Reed. His mouth
engulfs the glass and crunches. I think of what my
dentist would say, my beautiful gold caps . . .

Nov. 19. . . . I ask Kate where Sobaka is, she pre-
tends not to hear. Skip tells me later he was friend
of Khrush., hung on for while, now non-person. I
miss him. My strange weakness for cops and assas-
sins: their sense of craftsmanship?

III

Nov. 1. Off to Caucasus with Skip, Mrs. R., Kate. Fog,
no planes for twenty-four hours. Airport crammed
with hordes of sleeping. Soldiers, peasants, an epic
patience. Sleeping on clothy heaps of each other,
no noise of complaint. Many types of soldier uni-
form, long coats. Kate after twelve hours bullies way
onto plane, pointing to me as Guest of the State,
fierce performance. Engines screaming, officials
screaming, she screaming. Get on plane at 2 A.M.,
amid bundles, chickens, gypsies, sit opposite pair of
plump fortune tellers who groan and (very discreetly) throw up all the way to Tbilisi. Ears ache
in descent; no pressurization. Birds in airport, in
and out, remind of San Juan. Happy, sleepless. Sun
on hills, flowers like oleanders. Hotel as in Florida
Keys in Bogart movies, sour early morning service,

a bracing sense of the sinister. Great fist-shaking
Lenin statue in traffic circle. Flies buzz in room.

Nov. 2. Slept till noon. Reynolds wakes with phone
call. He and Mrs. caught later plane. Cowboys and
Indians, even my escorts have escorts. We go in two
cars to Pantheon on hill, Georgian escort lantern-
jawed professor of aesthetics. Cemetery full of funny
alphabet, big stone he says with almost tear in eye
called simply "Mother." Reynolds clues me sotto
voce it's Stalin's mother. Had been statue of S. here
so big it killed two workmen when they pulled it
down. Supper with many Georgian poets, toasts in
white wine, my own keep calling them "Russians"
which Kate corrects in translation to "Georgians."
Author of epic infatuated with Mrs. R., strawberry
blonde from Wisconsin, puts hands on thighs, kisses
throat, Skip grins sheepishly, what he's here for, to
improve relations. Cable car down the mountain,
Tbilisi a-spangle under us, all drunk, singing done in
pit of throat, many vibrations, hillbilly mournfulness,
back to bed. Same flies buzz.

Nov. 3. Car ride to Muxtyeta, oldest church in Chris-
tendom, professor of aesthetics ridicules God,
chastity, everybody winces. Scaldingly clear blue
sky, church a ruddy octagonal ruin with something
ancient and pagan in the center. Went to lunch with
snowy-haired painter of breasts. These painters of
a sleazy ethnic softness, of flesh like pastel landscapes, landscapes like pastel flesh. Where are the

real artists, the cartoonists who fill *Krokodil* with fanged bankers and cadaverous Adenauers, the anonymous Chardins of industrial detail? Hidden from me, like missile sites and working ports. Of the Russian cake they give me only frosting. By train to Armenia. We all share a four-bunk sleeper. Ladies undress below me, see Kate's hand dislodge beige buttoned canvasy thing, see circlet of lace flick past Ellen Reynolds's pale round knee. Closeted with female flesh and Skip's supercilious snore expect to stay awake, but fall asleep in top bunk like child among nurses. Yerevan station at dawn. The women, puffy-eyed and mussed, claim night of total insomnia. Difficulty of women sleeping on trains, boats, where men are soothed. Distrust of machinery? Sexual stimulation, Claire saying she used to come just from sitting on vibrating subway seat, never the IRT, only the IND. Took at least five stops.

Nov. 4. Svartz-Notz. Armenian cathedral. Old bones in gold bands. Our escort has withered arm, war record, dear smile, writing long novel about 1905 uprising. New city pink and mauve stone, old one Asiatic heaped rubble. Ruins of Alexander's palace, passed through on way to India. Gorgeous gorge.

Nov. 5. Lake Sevan, grim gray sulphuric beach, lowered lake six feet to irrigate land. Land dry and rosy. Back at hotel, man stopped in lobby, recognized me, here from Fresno visiting relatives, said he couldn't finish *The Chosen,* asked for autograph. Dinner with

Armenian science fiction writers, Kate in her element, they want to know if I know Ray Bradbury, Marshall McLuhan, Vance Packard, Mitchell Wilson. I don't. Oh. I say I know Norman Podhoretz and they ask if he wrote *Naked and Dead.*

Nov. 6. Long drive to "working" monastery. Two monks live in it. Chapel carved from solid rock, bushes full of little strips of cloth, people make a wish. Kate borrows my handkerchief, tears off strip, ties to bush, make a wish. Blushes when I express surprise. Ground littered with sacrificial bones. In courtyard band of farmers having ceremonial cookout honoring birth of son. Insist we join them, Reynoldses tickled pink, hard for American diplomats to get to clambake like this, real people. Priest scruffy sly fellow with gold fangs in beard. Armenians all wearing sneakers, look like Saroyan characters. Flies in wine, gobbets of warm lamb, blessings, toasts heavily directed toward our giggling round-kneed strawberry-blonde Ellen R. As we left we glimpsed real monk, walking along tumbledown parapet. Unexpectedly young. Pale, expressionless, very remote. A spy? Dry lands make best saints. Reynoldses both sick from effects of peoples' feast, confined to hotel while Kate and I, hardened sinners, iron stomachs, go to dinner with white-haired artist, painter of winsome faces, sloe eyes, humanoid fruit, etc.

Nov. 7. Woke to band music; today Revolution Day.

Should be in Red Square, but Kate talked me out of it. Smaller similar parade here, in square outside hotel. Overlook while eating breakfast of blini and caviar parade of soldiers, red flags, equipment enlarging phallically up to rockets, then athletes in different colors like gumdrops, swarm at end of children, people, citizens, red dresses conspicuous. Kate kept clucking tongue and saying she hates war. Reynoldses still rocky, hardly eat. Ellen admires my digestive toughness, I indifferent to her praise. Am I falling in love with Kate? Feel insecure away from her side, listen to her clear throat and toss in hotel room next to me. We walk in sun, I jostle to get between her and withered arm, jealous when they talk in Rooski, remember her blush when she tied half my torn hanky to that supernatural bush. What was her wish? Time to leave romantic Armenia. Back to Moscow by ten, ears ache fearfully in descent. Bitter cold, dusting of snow. Napoleon trembles.

IV

This sample letter, never sent, was found enclosed in the journal. "Claire" appears to have been the predecessor, in Bech's affections, of Miss Norma Latchett. Reprinted by permission, all rights © Henry Bech.

Dear Claire:

I am back in Moscow, after three days in Leningrad, an Italian opera set begrimed by years in an arctic warehouse and populated by a million out-of-work baritone villains. Today, the American Ambassador gave me a dinner to which no Russians came, because of something they think we did in the Congo, and I spent the whole time discussing shoes with Mrs. Ambassador, who hails originally, as she put it, from Charleston. She even took her shoe off so I could hold it—it was strange, warm, small. How are you? Can you feel my obsolete ardor? Can you taste the brandy? I live luxuriously, in the hotel where visiting plenipotentiaries from the Emperor of China are lodged, and Arabs in white robes leave oil trails down the hall. There may be an entire floor of English homosexual defectors, made over on the model of Cambridge digs. Lord, it's lonely, and bits of you—the silken depression beside each ankle-bone, the downy rhomboidal small of your back— pester me at night as I lie in exiled majesty, my laborious breathing being taped by threescore OGPU rookies. You were so beautiful. What happened? Was it all me, my fearful professional gloom, my Flaubertian syphilitic impotence? Or was it your shopgirl go-go brass, that held like a pornographic novel in a bureau (your left nipple was the drawer pull) a Quaker A-student from Darien? We turned each other inside out, it seemed to me, and made all those steak restaurants in the East Fifties light up like seraglios under bombardment. I will never be so young again. I am transported around here like a brittle curio; plug me into the nearest socket and I spout red, white, and blue. The Soviets like

me because I am redolent of the oppressive thirties.
I like them for the same reason. You, on the other
hand, were all sixties, a bath of sequins and glowing
pubic tendrils. Forgive my unconscionable distance,
our preposterous prideful parting, the way our mi-
raculously synchronized climaxes came to nothing,
like novae. Oh, I send you such airmail lost love,
Claire, from this very imaginary place, the letter may
beat the plane home, and jump into your refrigerator, and nestle against the illuminated parsley as if
we had never said unforgivable things.

H.

*Folded into the letter, as a kind of postscript, a pic-
ture postcard. On the obverse, in bad color, a picture of an iron statue, male. On the reverse, this
message:*

Dear Claire: What I meant to
say in my unsent letter was that
you were so good to me, good for
me, there was a goodness in me you
brought to birth. Virtue is so rare,
I thank you forever. The man on the
other side is Mayokovsky, who shot
himself and thereby won Stalin's un-
dying love. Henry

*Gay with Sputnik stamps, it passed through the
mails uncensored and was waiting for him when he
at last returned from his travels and turned the key
of his stifling, airless, unchanged apartment. It lay on*

the floor, strenuously cancelled. Claire had slipped it under the door. The lack of any accompanying note was eloquent. They never communicated again, though for a time Bech would open the telephone directory to the page where her number was encircled and hold it on his lap.—ED.

APPENDIX B

Bibliography

1. Books by Henry Bech (b. 1923, d. 19—)

Travel Light, novel. New York: The Velum Press, 1955. London: J. J. Goldschmidt, 1957.

Brother Pig, novella. New York: The Velum Press, 1957. London: J. J. Goldschmidt, 1958.

When the Saints, miscellany. [*Contents:* "Uncles and Dybbuks," "Subway Gum," "A Vote For Social Unconsciousness," "Soft-Boiled Sergeants," "The Vanishing Wisecrack," "Graffiti," "Sunsets Over Jersey," "The *Arabian Nights* At Your Own Pace," "Orthodoxy and Orthodontics," "Rag Bag" [collection of book reviews], "Displeased in the Dark" [collection of cinema reviews], forty-three untitled paragraphs under the head of "Tumblers Clicking."] New York: The Velum Press, 1958.

The Chosen, novel. New York: The Velum Press, 1963. London: J. J. Goldschmidt, 1963.

The Best of Bech, anthology. London: J. J. Goldschmidt, 1968. [Contains *Brother Pig* and selected essays from *When the Saints.*]

Think Big, novel. [In progress.]

2. Uncollected Articles and Short Stories

"Stee-raight'n Yo' Shoulduhs, Boy!", *Liberty*, XXXIV.33 (August 21, 1943) 62–63.

"Home for Hanukkah," *Saturday Evening Post*, CCXVII.2 (January 8, 1944) 45–46, 129–133.

"Kosher Konsiderations," *Yank*, IV.4 (January 26, 1944) 6.

"Rough Crossing," *Collier's*, XLIV (February 22, 1944) 23–25.

"London Under Buzzbombs," *New Leader*, XXVII.11 (March 11, 1944) 9.

"The Cockney Girl," *Story*, XIV.3 (May–June, 1944) 68–75.

"V-Mail from Brooklyn," *Saturday Evening Post*, CCXVII.25 (June 31, 1944) 28–29, 133–137.

"Letter from Normandy," *New Leader*, XXVII.29 (July 15, 1944) 6.

"Hey, Yank!", *Liberty*, XXXV.40 (September 17, 1944) 48–49.

"Letter from the Bulge," *New Leader*, XXVIII.1 (January 3, 1945) 6.

"Letter from the Reichstag," *New Leader*, XXVIII.23 (June 9, 1945) 4.

"Fraulein, kommen Zie hier, bitte," *The Partisan Review*, XII (October, 1945) 413–431.

"Rubble" [poem], *Tomorrow*, IV.7 (December, 1945) 45.

"Soap" [poem], *The Nation*, CLXII (June 22, 1946) 751.

"Ivan in Berlin," *Commentary*, I.5 (August, 1946) 68–77.

"Jig-a-de-Jig," *Liberty*, XXVII.47 (October 15, 1946) 38–39.

"Novels from the Wreckage," *New York Times Book Review*, LII (January 19, 1947) 6.

☞*The bulk of Bech's reviews, articles, essays, and prose-poems 1947–58 were reprinted in* When the Saints *(see above). Only exceptions are listed below.*

"My Favorite Reading in 1953," *New York Times Book Review*, LXVII (December 25, 1953) 2.

Appendix B

"Smokestacks" [poem], *Poetry*, LXXXIV.5 (August, 1954) 249–50.

"*Larmes d'huile*" [poem], *Accent*, XV.4 (Autumn, 1955) 101.

"Why I Will Vote for Adlai Stevenson Again" [part of paid political advertisement printed in various newspapers], October, 1956.

"My Favorite Salad," *McCall's*, XXXIV.4 (April, 1957) 88.

"Nihilistic? Me?" [interview with Lewis Nichols], *New York Times Book Review*, LXI (October 12, 1957) 17–18, 43.

"Rain King for a Day," *New Republic*, CXL.3 (January 19, 1959) 22–23.

"The Eisenhower Years: Instant Nostalgia," *Esquire*, LIV.8 (August, 1960) 54–61.

"Lay Off, Norman," *The New Republic*, CXLI.22 (May 14, 1960) 19–20.

"Bogie: The Tic That Told All," *Esquire*, LV.10 (October, 1960) 44–45, 108–111.

"The Landscape of Orgasm," *House and Garden*, XXI.3 (December, 1960) 136–141.

"Superscrew," *Big Table*, II.3 (Summer, 1961) 64–79.

"The Moth on the Pin," *Commentary*, XXXI (March, 1961) 223–224.

"Iris and Muriel and Atropos," *New Republic*, CXLIV.20 (May 15, 1961) 16–17.

"M-G-M and the U.S.A.," *Commentary*, XXXII (October, 1961) 305–316.

"My Favorite Christmas Carol," *Playboy*, VIII.12 (December, 1961) 289.

"The Importance of Beginning with a B: Barth, Borges, and Others," *Commentary*, XXXIII (February, 1962) 136–142.

"Down in Dallas" [poem], *New Republic*, CXLVI.49 (December 2, 1963) 28.

"My Favorite Three Books of 1963," *New York Times Book Review*, LXVII (December 19, 1963) 2.

"Daniel Fuchs: An Appreciation," *Commentary*, XLI.2 (February, 1964) 39–45.

"Silence," *The Hudson Review*, XVII (Summer, 1964) 258–275.

"Rough Notes from Tsardom," *Commentary*, XLI.2 (February, 1965) 39–47.

"Frightened Under Kindly Skies" [poem], *Prairie Schooner*, XXXIX.2 (Summer, 1965) 134.

"The Eternal Feminine As It Hits *Me*" [contribution to a symposium], *Rogue*, III.2 (February, 1966) 69.

"What Ever Happened to Jason Honeygale?" *Esquire*, LXI.9 (September, 1966) 70–73, 194–198.

"Romanticism Under Truman: A Reminiscence," *New American Review*, III (April, 1968) 59–81.

"My Three Least Favorite Books of 1968," *Book World*, VI (December 20, 1968) 13.

3. Critical Articles Concerning (Selected List)

Prescott, Orville, "More Dirt," *New York Times*, October 12, 1955.

Weeks, Edward, "*Travel Light* Heavy Reading," *Atlantic Monthly*, CCI.10 (October, 1955) 131–132.

Kirkus Service, Virginia, "Search for Meaning in Speed," XXIV (October 11, 1955).

Time, "V-v-vrooom!", LXXII.17 (October 12, 1955) 98.

Macmanaway, Fr. Patrick X., "Spiritual Emptiness Found Behind Handlebars," *Commonweal*, LXXII.19 (October 12, 1955) 387–388.

Engels, Jonas, "Consumer Society Burlesqued," *Progressive*, XXI.35 (October 20, 1955) 22.

Kazin, Alfred, "Triumphant Internal Combustion," *Commentary*, XXIX (December, 1955) 90–96.

Time, "Puzzling Porky," LXXIV.3 (January 19, 1957) 75.

Hicks, Granville, "Bech Impressive Again," *Saturday Review*, XLIII.5 (January 30, 1957) 27–28.

Appendix B

Callagan, Joseph, S.J., "Theology of Despair Dictates Dark Allegory," *Critic*, XVII.7 (February 8, 1957) 61–62.

West, Anthony, "Oinck, Oinck," *New Yorker*, XXXIII.4 (March 14, 1957) 171–173.

Steiner, George, "Candide as Schlemiel," *Commentary*, XXV (March, 1957) 265–270.

Maddocks, Melvin, "An Unmitigated Masterpiece," *New York Herald Tribune Book Review*, February 6, 1957.

Hyman, Stanley Edgar, "Bech Zeroes In," *New Leader*, XLII.9 (March 1, 1957) 38.

Poore, Charles, "Harmless Hodgepodge," *New York Times*, August 19, 1958.

Marty, Martin, "Revelations Within the Secular," *Christian Century*, LXXVII (August 20, 1958) 920.

Aldridge, John, "Harvest of Thoughtful Years," Kansas City *Star*, August 17, 1958.

Time, "Who Did the Choosing?" LXXXIII.26 (May 24, 1962) 121.

Klein, Marcus, "Bech's Mighty Botch," *Reporter*, XXX.13 (May 23, 1962) 54.

Thompson, John, "So Bad It's Good," *New York Review of Books*, II.14 (May 15, 1962) 6.

Dilts, Susan, "Sluggish Poesy, Murky Psychology," Baltimore *Sunday Sun*, May 20, 1962.

Miller, Jonathan, "Oopsie!", *Show*, III.6 (June, 1962) 49–52.

Macdonald, Dwight, "More in Sorrow," *Partisan Review*, XXVIII (Summer, 1962) 271–279.

Kazin, Alfred, "Bech's Strange Case Reopened," *Evergreen Review*, VII.7 (July, 1962) 19–24.

Podhoretz, Norman, "Bech's Noble Novel: A Case Study in the Pathology of Criticism," *Commentary*, XXXIV (October, 1962) 277–286.

Gilman, Richard, "Bech, Gass, and Nabokov: The Territory Beyond Proust," *Tamarack Review*, XXXIII.1 (Winter, 1963) 87–99.

Minnie, Moody, "Myth and Ritual in Bech's Evocations of

Lust and Nostalgia," *Wisconsin Studies in Contemporary Literature*, V.2 (Winter–Spring, 1964) 1267–1279.

Terral, Rufus, "Bech's Indictment of God," *Spiritual Rebels in Post-Holocaustal Western Literature*, ed. Webster Schott (Las Vegas: University of Nevada Press, 1964).

L'Heureux, Sister Marguerite, "The Sexual Innocence of Henry Bech," *America*, CX (May 11, 1965) 670–674.

Brodin, Pierre, "Henri Bech, le juif réservé," *Écrivains Americains d'aujourd'hui*" (Paris: N.E.D., 1965).

Elbek, Leif, "Damer og dæmoni," *Vindrosen*, Copenhagen, (January–February, 1965) 67–72.

Wagenbach, Dolf, "Bechkritic und Bechwissenschaft," *Neue Rundschau*, Frankfurt am Main, September–January, 1965–1966) 477–481.

Fiedler, Leslie, "*Travel Light:* Synopsis and Analysis," *E-Z Outlines*, No. 403 (Akron, O.: Hand-E Student Aids, 1966).

Tuttle, L. Clark, "Bech's Best Not Good Enough," *The Observer* (London), April 22, 1968.

Steinem, Gloria, "What Ever Happened to Henry Bech?", *New York*, II.46 (November 14, 1969) 17–21.

A Note About the Author

JOHN UPDIKE was born in 1932 in Shillington, Pennsylvania, and attended Harvard College and the Ruskin School of Drawing and Fine Arts in Oxford, England. From 1955 to 1957 he was a staff member of The New Yorker, *to which he has contributed stories, essays, and poems. He is the author of nine books of fiction and three of poetry, as well as a collection of essays and four small juvenile books.*